THE PHANTOM COACH

Thirteen Journeys into the Unknown

Collections by the same editor
THE HAUNTED SEA
UNDESIRABLE PROPERTIES

THE
PHANTOM COACH

Thirteen Journeys into the Unknown

Edited by
Peter C. Smith

WILLIAM KIMBER · LONDON

This collection first published in 1979 by
WILLIAM KIMBER & CO. LIMITED
Godolphin House, 22a Queen Anne's Gate,
London, SW1H 9AE

ISBN 0 7183 0276 1

© Peter C. Smith, 1979
Rick Ferreira, 1979
Mary Williams, 1979
Mrs James Turner, 1975
Peter Hackett, 1975
R. Chetwynd-Hayes, 1974
Alex Hamilton, 1964
The Estate of Ann Bridge, 1932
The Estate of E.F. Benson, 1923

97906064

0315154S

Photoset by
Specialised Offset Services Limited, Liverpool
and printed in Great Britain by
REDWOOD BURN LIMITED
Trowbridge & Esher

For
Colin Bussey

in memory of the New Mo, the Safari
and the way you tell 'em!

Contents

Acknowledgements

The editor would like to thank all those who have granted permission for stories within their copyright to be reprinted.

For 'No Ticket' by Mary Williams to the author.

For 'Silent Stowaway' by Rick Ferreira to the author.

For 'The Woman in Black' by Peter Hackett to the author.

For 'Non-Paying Passengers' by R. Chetwynd-Hayes to the author.

For 'Love Me, Love my Car' by James Turner to William Kimber & Co Ltd (From *The Way Shadows Fall*).

For 'The Attic Express' by Alex Hamilton to Jonathan Clowes Ltd (From *The Fourth Pan Book of Horror Stories*)

For 'In the Tube' by E.F. Benson to A.P. Watt & Son and the Estate of E.F. Benson (From *Visible and Invisible*)

For 'The Buick Saloon' by Ann Bridge to A.D. Peters & Co. Ltd. (From *The Song in the House*).

I

The Phantom Coach
Amelia Blandford Edwards

Amelia Blandford Edwards (1831-1892) was a very liberated Victorian lady who took an highly independent line at least a century before Germaine Greer. She travelled widely abroad, was a member of several research groups and wrote books on Egyptology as well as numerous short stories and novels. She was keenly involved in the suffrage issue for female rights and in deference to her this volume contains three other ghost tales by women writers!

The circumstances I am about to relate to you have truth to recommend them. They happened to myself, and my recollection of them is as vivid as if they had taken place only yesterday. Twenty years, however, have gone by since that night. During those twenty years I have told the story to but one other person. I tell it now with a reluctance which I find it difficult to overcome. All I entreat, meanwhile, is that you will abstain from forcing your own conclusions upon me. I want nothing explained away. I desire no arguments. My mind on this subject is quite made up, and, having the testimony of my own senses to rely upon, I prefer to abide by it.

Well! It was just twenty years ago, and within a day or two of the end of the grouse season. I had been out all day with my gun, and had had no sport to speak of. The wind was due east; the month, December; the place, a bleak wide moor in the far north of England. And I had lost my way. It was not a pleasant place in which to lose one's way, with the first feathery flakes of a coming snowstorm just fluttering down upon the heather, and the leaden evening closing in all around. I shaded my eyes with my hand, and stared anxiously into the gathering darkness, where the purple moorland melted into a range of low hills, some ten or twelve miles distant. Not the faintest smoke-wreath, not the tiniest cultivated patch, or fence, or sheep-track, met my eyes in any direction. There was nothing for it but to walk on, and take my chance of finding what shelter I could, by the way. So I shouldered my gun again, and pushed wearily forward; for I had been on foot since an hour after daybreak, and had eaten nothing since breakfast.

Meanwhile, the snow began to come down with ominous steadiness, and the wind fell. After this, the cold became more intense, and the night came rapidly up. As for me, my prospects darkened with the darkening sky, and my heart grew heavy as I thought how my young wife was already watching for me through the window of our little inn parlour, and thought of all the suffering in store for her throughout this weary night. We had been married four months, and, having spent our autumn in the Highlands, were now lodging in a remote little village situated just on the verge of the great English moorlands. We were very much in love, and, of course, very happy. This morning, when we parted, she had implored me to return before dusk, and I had promised her that I would. What would I not have given to have kept my word!

Even now, weary as I was, I felt that with a supper, an hour's rest, and a guide, I might still get back to her before midnight, if only guide and shelter could be found.

And all this time the snow fell and the night thickened. I stopped and shouted every now and then, but my shouts seemed only to make the silence deeper. Then a vague sense of uneasiness came upon me, and I began to remember stories of travellers who had walked on and on in the falling snow until, wearied out, they were fain to lie down and sleep their lives away. Would it be possible, I asked myself, to keep on thus through all the long dark night? Would there not come a time when my limbs must fail, and my resolution give way? When I, too, must sleep the sleep of death. Death! I shuddered. How hard to die just now, when life lay all so bright before me! How hard for my darling, whose whole loving heart – but that thought was not to be borne! To banish it, I shouted again, louder and longer, and then listened eagerly. Was my shout answered, or did I only fancy that I heard a far-off cry? I halloed again, and again the echo followed. Then a wavering speck of light came suddenly out of the dark, shifting, disappearing, growing momentarily nearer and brighter. Running towards it at full speed, I found myself, to my great joy, face to face with an old man and a lantern.

'Thank God!' was the exclamation that burst involuntarily from my lips.

Blinking and frowning, he lifted his lantern and peered into my face.

'What for?' growled he, sulkily.

'Well – for you. I began to fear I should be lost in the snow.'

'Eh, then, folks do get cast away hereabouts fra' time to time, an' what's to hinder you from bein' cast away likewise, if the Lord's so minded?'

'If the Lord is so minded that you and I shall be lost together, friend, we must submit,' I replied; 'but I don't mean to be lost without you. How far am I now from Dwolding?'

'A gude twenty mile, more or less.'

'And the nearest village?'

'The nearest village is Wyke, an' that's twelve mile t'other side.'

'Where do you live, then?'

'Out yonder,' said he, with a vague jerk of the lantern.

'You're going home, I presume?'

'Maybe I am.'

'Then I'm going with you.'

The old man shook his head, and rubbed his nose reflectively with the handle of the lantern.

'It ain't no use,' growled he. 'He 'on't let you in – not he.'

'We'll see about that,' I replied, briskly. 'Who is He?'

'The master.'

'Who is the master?'

'That's nowt to you,' was the unceremonious reply.

'Well, well; you lead the way, and I'll engage that the master shall give me shelter and a supper tonight.'

'Eh, you can try him!' muttered my reluctant guide; and, still shaking his head, he hobbled, gnome-like, away through the falling snow. A large mass loomed up presently out of the darkness, and a huge dog rushed out, barking furiously.

'Is this the house?' I asked.

'Ay; it's the house. Down, Bey!' And he fumbled in his pocket for the key.

I drew up close behind him, prepared to lose no chance of entrance, and saw in the little circle of light shed by the lantern that the door was heavily studded with iron nails, like the door of a prison. In another minute he had turned the key and I had pushed past him into the house.

Once inside, I looked round with curiosity, and found myself in a great raftered hall, which served, apparently, a variety of uses. One end was piled to the roof with corn, like a barn. The other was stored with flour-sacks, agricultural implements, casks, and all kinds of miscellaneous lumber; while from the beams overhead hung rows of hams, flitches, and bunches of dried herbs for winter use. In the centre of the floor stood some huge object gauntly dressed in a dingy wrapping-cloth, and reaching half-way to the rafters. Lifting a corner of this cloth, I saw, to my surprise, a telescope of very considerable size, mounted on a rude movable platform, with four small wheels. The tube was made of painted wood, bound round with bands of metal, rudely fashioned; the speculum, so far as I could estimate its size in the dim light, measured at least fifteen inches in diameter. While I was yet examining the instrument, and asking myself whether it was not the work of some self-taught optician, a bell rang sharply.

'That's for you,' said my guide, with a malicious grin. 'Yonder's his room.'

He pointed to a low black door at the opposite side of the hall. I crossed over, rapped somewhat loudly, and went in, without waiting for an invitation. A huge, white-haired old man rose from a table covered with books and papers, and confronted me sternly.

'Who are you?' said he. 'How came you here? What do you want?'

'James Murray, barrister-at-law. On foot across the moor. Meat, drink, and sleep.'

He bent his bushy brows into a portentous frown.

'Mine is not a house of entertainment,' he said, haughtily. 'Jacob, how dared you admit this stranger?'

'I didn't admit him,' grumbled the old man. 'He followed

me over the moor, and shouldered his way in before me. I'm no match for six foot two.'

'And pray, sir, by what right have you forced an entrance into my house?'

'The same by which I should have clung to your boat, if I were drowning. The right of self-preservation.'

'Self-preservation?'

'There's an inch of snow on the ground already,' I replied, briefly, 'and it would be deep enough to cover my body before daybreak.'

He strode to the window, pulled aside a heavy black curtain, and looked out.

'It is true,' he said. 'You can stay, if you choose, till morning. Jacob, serve the supper.'

With this he waved me to a seat, resumed his own, and became at once absorbed in the studies from which I had disturbed him.

I placed my gun in a corner, drew a chair to the hearth, and examined my quarters at leisure. Smaller and less incongruous in its arrangements than the hall, this room contained, nevertheless, much to awaken my curiosity. The floor was carpetless. The whitewashed walls were in parts scrawled over with strange diagrams, and in others covered with shelves crowded with philosophical instruments, the uses of many of which were unknown to me. On one side of the fireplace, stood a bookcase filled with dingy folios; on the other, a small organ, fantastically decorated with painted carvings of mediæval saints and devils. Through the half-opened door of a cupboard at the farther end of the room, I saw a long array of geological specimens, surgical preparations, crucibles, retorts, and jars of chemicals; while on the mantelshelf beside me, amid a number of small objects, stood a model of the solar system, a small galvanic battery, and a microscope. Every chair had its burden. Every corner was heaped high with books. The very floor was littered over with maps, casts, papers, tracings, and learned lumber of all conceivable kinds.

I stared about me with an amazement increased by every fresh object upon which my eyes chanced to rest. So strange a room I had never seen; yet seemed it stranger still, to find such a room in a lone farmhouse amid those wild and solitary moors! Over and over again, I looked from my host to his surroundings, and from his surroundings back to my host, asking myself who and what he could be? His head was singularly fine; but it was more the head of a poet than of a philosopher. Broad in the temples, prominent over the eyes, and clothed with a rough profusion of perfectly white hair, it had all the ideality and much of the ruggedness that characterises the head of Louis von Beethoven. There were the same deep lines about the mouth, and the same stern furrows in the brow. There was the same concentration of expression. While I was yet observing him, the door opened, and Jacob brought in the supper. His master then closed his book, rose, and with more courtesy of manner than he had yet shown, invited me to the table.

A dish of ham and eggs, a loaf of brown bread, and a bottle of admirable sherry, were placed before me.

'I have but the homeliest farmhouse fare to offer you, sir,' said my entertainer. 'Your appetite, I trust, will make up for the deficiencies of our larder.'

I had already fallen upon the viands, and now protested, with the enthusiasm of a starving sportsman, that I had never eaten anything so delicious.

He bowed stiffly, and sat down to his own supper, which consisted, primitively, of a jug of milk and a basin of porridge. We ate in silence and, when we had done, Jacob removed the tray. I then drew my chair back to the fireside. My host, somewhat to my surprise, did the same, and turning abruptly towards me, said:

'Sir, I have lived here in strict retirement for three-and-twenty years. During that time, I have not seen as many strange faces, and I have not read a single newspaper. You are the first stranger who has crossed my threshold for more than four years. Will you favour me with a few words of information respecting that outer world from which I have parted company so long?'

'Pray interrogate me,' I replied. 'I am heartily at your service.'

He bent his head in acknowledgment; leaned forward, with his elbows resting on his knees and his chin supported in the palms of his hands; stared fixedly into the fire; and proceeded to question me.

His inquiries related chiefly to scientific matters, with the later progress of which, as applied to the practical purposes of life, he was almost wholly unacquainted. No student of science myself, I replied as well as my slight information permitted; but the task was far from easy, and I was much relieved when, passing from interrogation to discussion, he began pouring forth his own conclusions upon the facts which I had been attempting to place before him. He talked, and I listened spellbound. He talked till I believe he almost forgot my presence, and only thought aloud. I had never heard anything like it then; I have never heard anything like it since. By-and-by – I forget now by what link of conjecture or illustration – he passed on to that field which lies beyond the boundary line of even conjectural philosophy, and reaches no man knows whither. He spoke of the soul and its aspirations; of the spirit and its powers; of second sight; of prophecy; of those phenomena which, under the names of ghosts, spectres, and supernatural appearances, have been denied by the sceptics and attested by the credulous, of all ages.

'The world,' he said, 'grows hourly more and more sceptical of all that lies beyond its own narrow radius; and our men of science foster the fatal tendency. They condemn as fable all that resists experiment. They reject as false all that cannot be brought to the test of the laboratory or the dissecting-room. Against what superstition have they waged so long and obstinate a war as against the belief in apparitions? And yet what superstition has maintained its hold upon the minds of men so long and so firmly? Show me any fact in physics, in history, in archæology, which is supported by testimony so wide and so various. Attested by all races of men, in all ages, and in all climates, by the soberest sages of antiquity, by the rudest savage of today, by the Christian, the Pagan, the Pantheist, the Materialist, this phenomenon is treated as a nursery tale by the philosophers of our century. Circumstantial evidence weighs with them as a feather in the balance. The comparison of causes with effects, however valuable in psychical science, is put aside as worthless and unreliable. The evidence of competent witnesses, however conclusive in a court of justice, counts for nothing. He who pauses before he pronounces, is condemned as a trifler. He who believes, is a dreamer or a fool.'

He spoke with bitterness, and, having said this, relapsed for some minutes into silence. Presently he raised his head from his hands and added, with an altered voice and manner:

'I, sir, paused, investigated, believed, and was not ashamed to state my convictions to the world. I, too, was branded as a visionary, held up to ridicule by my contemporaries, and hooted from that field of science in which I had laboured with honour during all the best years of my life. These things happened just three-and-twenty years ago. Since then I have lived as you see me living now, and the world has forgotten me, as I have forgotten the world. You have my history.'

'It is a very sad one,' I murmured, scarcely knowing what to answer.

'It is a very common one,' he replied. 'I have only suffered for the truth, as many a better and wiser man has suffered before me.'

He rose, as if desirous of ending the conversation, and went over to the window.

'It has ceased snowing,' he observed, as he dropped the curtain and came back to the fireside.

'Ceased!' I exclaimed, starting eagerly to my feet. 'Oh, if it were only possible – but no! it is hopeless. Even if I could find my way across the moor, I could not walk twenty miles tonight.'

'Walk twenty miles tonight!' repeated my host. 'What are you thinking of?'

'Of my wife,' I replied impatiently. 'Of my young wife, who does not know that I have lost my way, and who is at this moment breaking her heart with suspense and terror.'

'Where is she?'

'At Dwolding, twenty miles away.'

'At Dwolding,' he echoed, thoughtfully. 'Yes, the distance, it is true, is twenty miles; but – are you so very anxious to save the next six or eight hours?'

'So very, very anxious that I would give ten guineas at this moment for a guide and a horse.'

'Your wish can be gratified at a less costly rate,' said he, smiling. 'The night mail from the north, which changes horses at Dwolding, passes within five miles of this spot, and will be due at a certain cross-road in about an hour and a quarter. If Jacob were to go with you across the moor, and put you into the old coach-road, you could find your way, I suppose, to where it joins the new one?'

'Easily – gladly.'

He smiled again, rang the bell, gave the old servant his directions, and, taking a bottle of whisky and a wineglass from the cupboard in which he kept his chemicals, said:

'The snow lies deep, and it will be difficult walking tonight on the moor. A glass of usquebaugh before you start?'

I would have declined the spirit, but he pressed it on me, and I drank it. It went down my throat like liquid flame, and almost took my breath away.

'It is strong,' he said; 'but it will help to keep out the cold. And now you have no moments to spare. Goodnight!'

I thanked him for his hospitality, and would have shaken hands, but that he had turned away before I could finish my sentence. In another minute I had traversed the hall, Jacob had locked the outer door behind me, and we were out on the wide white moor.

Although the wind had fallen, it was still bitterly cold. Not a star glimmered in the black vault overhead. Not a sound, save the rapid crunching of the snow beneath our feet, disturbed the heavy stillness of the night. Jacob, not too well pleased with his mission, shambled on before in sullen silence, his lantern in his hand, and his shadow at his feet. I followed, with my gun over my shoulder, as little inclined for conversation as himself. My thoughts were full of my late host. His voice yet rang in my ears. His eloquence yet held my imagination captive. I remember to this day, with surprise, how my over-excited brain retained whole sentences and parts of sentences, troops of brilliant images, and fragments of splendid reasoning, in the very words in which he had uttered them. Musing thus over what I had heard, and striving to recall a lost link here and there, I strode on at the heels of my guide, absorbed and unobservant. Presently – at the end, as it seemed to me, of only a few minutes – he came to a sudden halt, and said:

'Yon's your road. Keep the stone fence to your right hand, and you can't fail of the way.'

'This, then, is the old coach-road?'

'Ay, 'tis the old coach-road.'

'And how far do I go, before I reach the cross-roads?'

'Nigh upon three mile.'

I pulled out my purse, and he became more communicative.

'The road's a fair road enough,' said he, 'for foot passengers; but 'twas over steep and narrow for the northern traffic. You'll mind where the parapet's broken away, close again the sign-post. It's never been mended since the accident.'

'What accident?'

'Eh, the night mail pitched right over into the valley below – a gude fifty feet an' more – just at the worst bit o' road in the whole country.'

'Horrible! Were many lives lost?'

'All. Four were found dead, and t'other two died next morning.'

'How long is it since this happened?'

'Just nine year.'

'Near the sign-post, you say? I will bear it in mind. Goodnight.'

'Gude-night, sir, and thankee.' Jacob pocketed his half-crown, made a faint pretence of touching his hat, and trudged back by the way he had come.

I watched the light of his lantern till it quite disappeared, and then turned to pursue my way alone. This was no longer matter of the slightest difficulty, for, despite the dead darkness overhead, the line of stone fence showed distinctly enough against the pale gleam of the snow. How silent it seemed now with only my footsteps to listen to; how silent and how solitary! A strange disagreeable sense of loneliness stole over me. I walked faster. I hummed a fragment of a tune. I cast up enormous sums in my head, and accumulated them at compound interest. I did my best, in short, to forget the startling speculations to which I had but just been listening, and, to some extent, I succeeded.

Meanwhile the night air seemed to become colder and colder, and though I walked fast I found it impossible to keep myself warm. My feet were like ice. I lost sensation in my hands, and grasped my gun mechanically. I even breathed with difficulty, as though, instead of traversing a quiet north country highway, I were scaling the uppermost heights of some gigantic Alp. This last symptom became presently so distressing, that I was forced to stop for a few minutes and lean against the stone fence. As I did so, I chanced to look back up the road, and there, to my infinite relief, I saw a distant point of light, like the gleam of an approaching lantern. I at first concluded that Jacob had retraced his steps and followed me; but even as the conjecture presented itself, a second light flashed into sight – a light evidently parallel with the first, and approaching at the same rate of motion. It needed no second thought to show me that these must be the carriage-lamps of some private vehicle, though it seemed strange that it should take a road professedly disused and dangerous.

There could be no doubt, however, of the fact, for the lamps grew larger and brighter every moment, and I even fancied I could already see the dark outline of the carriage between them. It was coming up very fast, and quite noiselessly, the snow being nearly a foot deep under the wheels.

And now the body of the vehicle became distinctly visible behind the lamps. It looked strangely lofty. A sudden suspicion flashed upon me. Was it possible that I had passed the cross-roads in the dark without observing the sign-post, and could this be the very coach which I had come to meet?

No need to ask myself that question a second time, for here it came round the bend of the road, guard and driver, one outside passenger, and four steaming greys, all wrapped in a soft haze of light, through which the lamps blazed out, like a pair of fiery meteors.

I jumped forward, waved my hat, and shouted. The mail came down at full speed, and passed me. For a moment I feared that I had not been seen or heard, but it was only for a moment. The coachman pulled up; the guard, muffled to the eyes in capes and comforters, and apparently sound asleep in the rumble, neither answered my hail nor made the slightest effort to dismount; the outside passenger did not even turn his head. I opened the door for myself, and looked in. There were but three travellers inside, so I stepped in, shut the door, slipped into the vacant corner, and congratulated myself on my good fortune.

The atmosphere of the coach seemed, if possible, colder than that of the outer air, and was pervaded by a singularly damp and disagreeable smell. I looked round at my fellow-passengers. They were all three men and all silent. They did not seem to be asleep, but each leaned back in his corner of the vehicle, as if absorbed in his own reflections. I attempted to open a conversation.

'How intensely cold it is tonight,' I said, addressing my opposite neighbour.

He lifted his head, looked at me, but made no reply.

'The winter,' I added, 'seems to have begun in earnest.'

Although the corner in which he sat was so dim that I could distinguish none of his features very clearly, I saw that his eyes were still turned full upon me. And yet he answered never a word.

At any other time I should have felt, and perhaps expressed, some annoyance, but at the moment I felt too ill to do either. The icy coldness of the night air had struck a chill to my very marrow, and the strange smell inside the coach was affecting me with an intolerable nausea. I shivered from head to foot, and turning to my left-hand neighbour, asked if he had any objection to an open window.

He neither spoke nor stirred.

I repeated the question somewhat more loudly, but with the same result. Then I lost patience, and let the sash down. As I did so, the leather strap broke in my hand, and I observed that the glass was covered with a thick coat of mildew, the accumulation, apparently, of years. My attention being thus drawn to the condition of the coach, I examined it more narrowly, and saw by the uncertain light of the outer lamps that it was in the last stage of dilapidation. Every part of it was not only out of repair, but in a condition of decay. The sashes splintered at a touch. The leather fittings were crusted over with mould, and literally rotting from the woodwork. The floor was almost breaking away beneath my feet. The whole machine, in short, was foul with damp, and had evidently been dragged from some outhouse in which it had been mouldering away for years, to do another day or two of duty on the road.

I turned to the third passenger, whom I had not yet addressed, and hazarded one more remark.

'This coach,' I said, 'is in a deplorable condition. The regular mail, I suppose, is under repair?'

He moved his head slowly, and looked me in the face, without speaking a word. I shall never forget that look while I live. I turned cold at heart under it. I turn cold at heart even now when I recall it. His eyes glowed with a fiery unnatural lustre. His face was livid as the face of a corpse. His bloodless lips were drawn back as if in the agony of death, and showed the gleaming teeth between.

The words that I was about to utter died upon my lips, and a strange horror – a dreadful horror – came upon me. My sight had by this time become used to the gloom of the coach, and I could see with tolerable distinctness. I turned to my opposite neighbour. He, too, was looking at me, with the same startling pallor in his face, and the same stony glitter in his eyes. I passed my hand across my brow. I turned to the passenger on the seat beside my own, and saw – oh Heaven! how shall I describe what I saw? I saw that he was no living man – that none of them were living men, like myself! A pale phosphorescent light – the light of putrefaction – played upon their awful faces; upon their hair, dank with the dews of the grave; upon their clothes, earth-stained and dropping to pieces; upon their hands, which were as the hands of corpses long buried. Only their eyes, their terrible eyes, were living; and those eyes were all turned menacingly upon me!

A shriek of terror, a wild unintelligible cry for help and mercy, burst from my lips as I flung myself against the door, and strove in vain to open it.

In that single instant, brief and vivid as a landscape beheld in the flash of summer lightning, I saw the moon shining down through a rift of stormy cloud – the ghastly sign-post rearing its warning finger by the wayside – the broken parapet – the plunging horses – the black gulf below. Then, the coach reeled like a ship at sea. There came a mighty crash – a sense of crushing pain – and then darkness …

It seemed as if years had gone by when I awoke one

morning from a deep sleep, and found my wife watching by my bedside. I will pass over the scene that ensued, and give you, in half a dozen words, the tale she told me with tears of thanksgiving. I had fallen over a precipice, close against the junction of the old coach-road and the new, and had only been saved from certain death by lighting upon a deep snowdrift that had accumulated at the foot of the rock beneath. In this snowdrift I was discovered at daybreak, by a couple of shepherds, who carried me to the nearest shelter, and brought a surgeon to my aid. The surgeon found me in a state of raving delirium, with a broken arm and a compound fracture of the skull. The letters in my pocket-book showed my name and address; my wife was summoned to nurse me; and, thanks to youth and a fine constitution, I came out of danger at last. The place of my fall, I need scarcely say, was precisely that at which the north mail had a frightful accident nine years before.

I never told my wife the fearful events which I have just related to you. I told the surgeon who attended me; but he treated the whole adventure as a mere dream born of the fever in my brain. We discussed the question over and over again, until we found that we could discuss it with temper no longer, and then we dropped it. Others may form what conclusions they please – I *know* that twenty years ago I was the fourth inside passenger in that Phantom Coach.

II

Love me, Love my car
James Turner

James Turner wrote several masterly collections of ghost stories, as well as editing anthologies. Many of his stories were set in Cornwall where he lived and which with its unique atmosphere of by-gone ages inspires many writers in this genre. Here is one of his Cornish stories.

Love me, love my car, a heart-cry from a fanatic perhaps. Men, it is said, often treat their new motor with greater loving care and respect than they lavish on their spouse and family. In James Turner's story the car indeed exerts a powerful influence over its new owners, but is it love?

She liked the car at once. It was absurd, of course, to say that she had a feeling that it was waiting for her, but its radiator grille, generally grinning and ready to bite, it had always seemed to her, was slightly bent in the left hand corner. This gave the mouth, she thought, a pathetic look.

'I'm being anthropomorphic,' she said to herself, 'And it's damned silly over an old bit of iron and glass.' But she loved any chance to roll off her tongue such long words; to do so made her feel good and, God knows, being a librarian she had every chance to indulge her love of words, especially long words, never mind if people sometimes accused her of showing off.

The car was an Austin 'Countryman' of about 1965 which meant it just suited them for holidays, with being able to let down the back seat and make all that room inside for beds and things. Ted, her husband, opened the door and got in. 'Don't make 'em any longer,' he said, 'That's why it's cheap. Bit of rust, here and there, too, but that hardly matters. Do us for a year or so, I imagine.'

Actually he didn't tell her until they were packed up and on their way to Cornwall, that there was another reason for the low price. The car had been smashed up a bit in an accident in Rampart Street, Salisbury. It had been rebuilt in an amateur kind of way.

'Oh, Ted,' she said, 'Was it wise to buy it, then?' Conscious in her own mind that she herself was half responsible for their owning it, she being in her silly mood when they went to the car dealer in the Camberwell Road, after seeing it advertised in the evening paper. 'It looks pathetic,' she had said when Ted asked her there, in the yard, whether she liked it. 'Uncared for, like an old dog.'

'Don't be bloody stupid,' Ted replied. 'Get in and see if you like the feel of it.' And she had. At once she felt at home. The car seemed to respond to her.

Now Ted drew into a lay-by and, in answer to her question, produced an M.O.T. certificate of road-worthiness as well as a Guarantee from the salesman. 'Can't do more than that, can you? And we only had £150, so we could hardly have gone for something more ambitious. And she does go well, there's no denying.'

'I suppose the bent radiator grille is part of the accident?' she asked, pulling out a thermos and some sandwiches. 'Let's have lunch now.'

It wasn't the ideal place, a lay-by with traffic whizzing past at high speed, but she knew if Ted drove on he would be 'difficult' about finding a turning-off.

'I suppose so,' he said, happy that their first holiday as man and wife had begun. 'But I never noticed it.'

The weather that September was blazing. Summer had come suddenly and late. It was unbelievable, only, of course, the nights were drawing in. They parked the car on a headland, out of St Agnes, amongst some gorse and heather, a sort of secret place.

The 'season' was almost over and there was no other car in sight. In the heat of the afternoon they ran down the cliff path to the sea below, through the quickset hedges and ling and gorse, laughing like two children (they were not much more). They undressed and positively flung themselves into the sea which seemed almost to be waiting for them, for their youth and gaiety. Meg, born and bred in London, had never seen anything like it. The sea, smooth and opalescent, the mauve-grey rocks, the impossible beauty of sand-pools and the light created by the beneficent September sun were so beyond her expectations that she wanted to wriggle herself into the soft sand, become a part of it. The shells she picked up, ordinary to most people, were, to her, a wonder beyond belief. Above all she wanted to possess it so that the pictures, the feel of the seascape, the clouds and the sea itself, would never leave her. She was ecstatic and speechless and Ted, who was a Cornishman, born in Penzance, looked at her and loved her twice as much.

Meg kept to the shallow water near the rocks where the small waves came in and washed the shells bright again. She wasn't, anyway, a brilliant swimmer but Ted, who was, swam out into the bay, round a headland and out of her sight. The heat of the afternoon was terrific and she was beginning to be sunburnt. The moment she began to be apprehensive for Ted's safety, he appeared round the headland rocks and swam into her, lying gasping on the sand, pretending to be exhausted.

She ran to help him, uttering little cries. He caught her and pulled her to the wet sand, laughing at her distress. He didn't understand her sudden anger, or the way she slapped him in her relief.

'Don't ever do that again,' she said.

'What, darling?'

'Swim out of my sight and pretend to be half dead when you come in. I can't bear it. I won't bear it.' She picked up a length of wet seaweed and began lashing him with it as if he were a naughty child.

'Darling, darling,' he laughed and clung to her in her fury. 'I adore you. I promise never to play the fool again.' He picked her up and carried her to her place beside the deep rock pool. She was laughing happily now. He threw her into the water and followed her. Neither of them had been so happy since the day they were married a year ago.

When they were drying themselves in the late afternoon sun, Ted said, 'Tell you what. We won't try to find digs or an hotel. Let's stay with the car. There's plenty of food, isn't there?' She nodded sleepily, curled in the warm sand, the sea soothing her, her whole body melting in the in-and-out sighing of the tide. 'And there'll be a moon. We can bathe by moonlight, like I used to as a kid.'

They stayed on the sand until they were hungry and then began the climb back to the cliff-top and the car. When they emerged from the cliff path and the stretch of sward was between them and the car, Ted let out a yell. He began running, shouting, 'Get out of there. What the bloody hell ...'

Meg, who had caught her dress on a whip of grass and was bending over to unloose it, was astonished at what he was doing. He seemed suddenly to have gone mad. Actually she began laughing at the picture of Ted running towards the car waving his arms and shouting at non-existent people. At least she could see no one. She released her dress with only a small tear and ran across the grass to him.

'Whatever's the matter,' she panted out, coming up to the dark car. 'What's all the fuss about? Sheep or something?'

'Sheep nothing.' Ted said shame-facedly.

'Well, why all the shouting and carry on? Do you want all Cornwall to know you're back in the land of your fathers?' She thrust her long hair out of her eyes, that hair which, in the deep pool, had made her imagine she was a mermaid. Suddenly, as she bent her head backwards, Ted could see the moon reflected in her iris. 'Oh, it was nothing, I suppose. Some trick of the moonlight. Or the country. Or the sea.'

'Well, what trick? You must have thought something was up or you wouldn't have pulled the back of the car open.'

'It was lovers.'

'Lovers? What on earth do you mean?'

'In the back of the car.'

'Don't be silly. I saw nobody and I was right behind you. There was nobody. I don't suppose there's anybody for miles. You were dreaming. All that sun and sea water, that's what's the matter with you.'

'It was when I came off the cliff path. There was a light on in the car, you know the inside light, and a couple were in the back, making love. I heard them. Bloody cheek! In our car.'

'But, Ted, look. The back seat is still up in position. That only gives them, whoever it was, a tiny space. To make love you'd need that seat flat. That's the point of the car, isn't it?'

'I don't care how much space they had, they were there. I saw them, a girl with golden hair and a man with a beard. Right on top of her. She was struggling and hitting him.'

'Well, where are they now? They couldn't have got far.' She laughed. 'You've got love-making on the brain, like all men.'

'How the hell do I know where they are? They'd gone when I reached the car and the inside light was off.'

Meg began to busy herself with making supper. She stood beside the car. 'There isn't anyone for miles,' she said again, as if to convince herself. 'Here, have some coffee, do you good.'

They sat by the car (a haven of safety in the surrounding night) and listened to the sounds of silence, the insect noises in the grass, the movement of small animals in the gorse and bracken. Where the cliff edge began to group down to the sea the light was mauve, the gorse tipped with yellow moonlight, the interior of the quick hedges black and still. A little knot of old man's beard, gone to seed, was like gossamer on the thick hedge. Someone might have left cotton wool about.

They put their arms round each other in the primal loneliness of the early night and let the sound of the sea come up to them, her small round face beside his, 'It's bliss,' she whispered. 'The quiet is bliss.' She was half asleep against the car and her husband. She was thinking and hearing in her head the sound of trains over a viaduct near their home in London. Suddenly she realised that tonight was the first time she was hearing them when they weren't there. So accustomed had she become to them. 'No trains,' she said dreamily, 'no trains at all.'

It was their first adventure together, there beside the car on the cliff top beyond the road, in their secret place, with the pineapply smell of the gorse about them and the winking light of a lighthouse miles away. Vaguely she heard Ted say, 'It will be Trevose Head. Shouldn't think there'll be much danger with the sea so calm and the night so bright and warm.' Later he got up and stretched. 'I'm going down for a last dip,' he said, 'What about you?'

The moon was now huge in the mauve sky. The earth was giving off a heat which surrounded them like a blanket. The mouth of the path through the bracken and gorse was black with shadow and, in the field across the road behind the car, sheep were snuffling and pulling grass in the half-light.

'It's magical,' Meg said, falling sideways on to the grass, looking up at the moon, her mouth open with the pleasure of it. She had never been in the country at night in her life, to say nothing of being half in country and half in sea. Though she had often watched the moonlight over the London roofs from her bedroom in Streatham, it was nothing like this, nothing so pure as this. The light, soft as it was, almost hurt her in its purity and lack of dust. It was like a very highly polished mirror; she could almost see herself in it.

'You go down,' she said, completely unafraid, 'I'll get the car ready to sleep in. It will be chilly later on, you see. You'll be glad of it. We've a lot of coats and rugs and things. I'll make up a bed. For real lovers this time.' She watched him disappear into the gorse and heard him call back. 'Won't be long and I'll take care' and then he was gone.

It was only then that the night, the dark unfamiliar places of the countryside created by the moon shadows, the cries of sea birds which she thought she heard and the distant winking of the lighthouse, made her suddenly afraid, suddenly aware that she was entirely alone and that if anyone were to come out of the dark headland scrub, Ted would be too far away to help her.

Now they began whispering to her, the things of night, now the tiny sounds of insect were voices calling to her. An enormous, hard-shelled beetle zoomed almost into her hair and banged its way through the dark night as if, she thought, it had come for her, she held her breasts in her hand as if the cattle would come out of the night to drink her milk, or the great Cornish Giant, Bedruthen, about which Ted had told her tales, was already striding in her direction, hollowing the earth with his huge footsteps. And the black hound slavering over the grass ...

She opened the back of the 'Countryman', pulled the seat down to make the large space behind the driving seat and crept in. She was safe under the tiny light of the car. It was like putting on armour. If things were moving in the dark gorse or across the sheep field, they could do her no harm here.

She hadn't realised she was so sleepy. When she had arranged the rugs and cushions they brought with them, she lay down, her feet out before her, pulled a raincoat over her shoulders and was fast asleep in a minute.

She must have been asleep an hour. She awoke with a start and felt herself pinned to the floor of the car.

'Ted,' she whispered dreamily, 'Darling, oh, darling,' and put up her arms to hold him, to love him. Sleepily she thought, he must have come back and crept in to the car not wanting to disturb her. It was quite dark inside the car because the moon was directly overhead. She could sense Ted's face coming down on hers, holding her head firmly, and then the hot mouth and the feel of hair. When she realised that the hair was a beard, she shrieked and tried to get up in the enclosed space at the back of the car. She was pushed down again. She felt the hands of the man pulling up her dress and the feel of naked limbs on hers and the man going in between her legs. She screamed again but the man's body bore down upon her and the words filled the car. 'Shut up, you little bitch. You've asked for it.'

'Ted,' she screamed again and flung out a hand towards the interior light and switched it on. For a second she saw him, a thin man with a beard, his lips wet, his mouth open, and then she was alone in the car. Now, when she looked out of the windows she could see the moonlight each side of the car, slices of yellow light stretching off into the country or out to sea. She shoved the back open and got out into the perfect night.

She was utterly alone. She was shivering with fright, her hands quivering in front of her, the bushes behind her full of menace and faces and obscene words. Yet there was nobody and, in her mind, she knew no one was there in the flesh. Yet, it had been so real, her attempted rape.

When Ted found her she was still standing beside the car shivering and weeping. He took her into his arms.

'Come on,' he said, comforting her, 'It's not all that late. Somewhere will be open. We'll find somewhere. We can't stay here.'

She quickly recovered and helped him to fix up the car. They drove into the nearest village. They were lucky. Pubs in Cornwall are few and far between. But this one – only a mile from the headland – was still open and they had a double room.

Later they were in each other's arms in bed and laughing. They were young enough not to be disturbed for long.

'It was your man with a beard,' Meg said, returned to her level-headedness. 'What a brute! He nearly raped me, Ted, he did proper.'

'Get away with you,' Ted said jokingly, though he had not been deceived by the condition he found Meg in when he came back from his moonlight bathe. She was dead scared, no doubt of it. All he wanted to do, then, was to calm her fears, smoothe them away. 'I don't know, darling,' he said, 'I certainly did see those two making love in the car. And now you say … damn him, I'd like to get my hands on him.'

'You'll never do that, dear. Whoever it was, he's dead. Oh, God, Ted, I can't explain it any more than you can.'

'It's probably got something to do with the place we put the car. Damn it, hundreds of people must have made love at that spot, it's so secret. Some trace still left?'

Meg looked up at the ceiling. She was warm, now, happy, her fears dispelled. The countryside had been destroyed. 'It was an incubus,' she said, conscious that she loved pronouncing the word, 'I know it was. I've read about them.'

'What in hell's that? You and your long words.'

'It's a spirit which makes love to a woman. Just as a succubus is a spirit which makes love to a man.'

'Get away with you,' Ted said again, putting his arms round her in the big double bed. 'The things you know! I'll have to try sleeping in the car alone. Might be fun.'

'Don't you dare, Ted Baxter,' Meg propped herself on an elbow and looked down at him. 'And, as of now, my lad, you can just stop making jokes about spirit lovers. I know you, you'll go on forever about them, boring everyone.'

Ted kissed her and fondled her and loved her. 'God bless you, honey, I can't keep awake any longer. But call me if this incubus thing comes again. I'll know how to deal with him.'

'Funny thing was, Ted,' she teased him in her relief and happiness. 'When I got over my fright I rather liked it. He wasn't bad.'

But Ted was asleep and never heard the remark.

She told herself, when the end came, that she should have realised what was going to happen. It was not that anything big, like her phantom lover, occurred again. Indeed, nothing marred the rest of their holiday. Yet a number of small things, the dog and the children and, idiotically, an old coat which she found in the car one day which didn't belong to either of them, should have warned her. In one sense they were part of the dark side of her experience and then, above all, on this wonderful holiday, she wanted light, of the sun, of the sea, of the spinning seagulls in the headland breezes. It was the absorption into this light which, she knew, was creating her even, perhaps, creating their child within her.

Maybe the first time she heard the children she did try to talk to Ted about it. But he only treated the whole thing as a joke.

'We've got a haunted car on our hands, darling,' he said, 'Bet that's never happened before.' And they had gone off, arm in arm, to the local pub for pasties and the wrestling in a field behind. Not that she worried, the weather was so fine and the days too full for worry. The holiday was slipping away so quickly and she had seen nothing but the immediate neighbourhood of the pub where, finally, they had agreed to stay.

The children hadn't been in the car, of course, not in the flesh anyway, she said to herself. Though when she first heard them and the noise they were making, she turned automatically, as if she were back in the library, and admonished them. A man's voice had said distinctly, 'Oh, let them be, Angela, it's a holiday. What does it matter how much noise they make?' and she had driven back to the pub from the bay where she went every morning before breakfast, leaving Ted still in bed.

She could not, then, resist the early morning light and the thought of the sea. In any case she wasn't sleepy and she had this morning, gone down to a small enclosed sandy bay and paddled, getting her feet into seaweed, walking amongst the rocks and idiotically waving to a huge boat on the horizon. No one else was on the untrodden sand except a great shaggy dog which paid no attention to her.

When she got back to the car and shut the door, the

children began shouting. Their voices came from the back, two girls and a boy. She wasn't at all frightened. The only odd thing was that when she arrived back for breakfast she looked into the back of the car and saw the signs of sandy feet on the floor. That sand hadn't been there the day before, she knew, because she had spent an hour cleaning out the car. She shut the door and went to find Ted, already eating cornflakes and drinking his coffee.

Now she was no longer frightened, though it was obvious to her that, at certain times, the car was haunted. She was completely certain of this the day the dog barked. It was at the same bay, at the same time of morning. She had driven down without Ted and it was all the same, though the sea was further out. Even the same dog was running on the sand, only quite some way from her, over towards a building which she knew had once been a fish cellar and was now converted into a house. It was empty and she explored it, looking in at the windows, half expecting to see faces. But, it being a holiday house, there was no one, only furniture and beds in cellophane covers piled one on top of the other. It looked and felt sad.

The dog was still running at the water's edge, chasing gulls, when she walked back, quite alone, picking up shells, pink scallops, tellins and cowries. When she shut the door of the car, however, she heard a dog bark from the back. It couldn't have been the dog on the beach, of course, for she looked at him out there immediately, still running after gulls, eternally hoping, eternally disappointed. She wasn't to be taken in again and did not turn round until she felt the rough tongue against her cheek. That took her by surprise and she jumped round only to see that the car was completely empty.

Later that day she made what she thought of as a discovery; not that it had much effect on her. Ted had gone into the sea from what she called her pre-breakfast beach. The whole wide bay was before her and she could see him swimming in the otherwise empty sea. She pulled open the glove cupboard and took the long, buff-coloured envelope out. Inside was the car's log-book which Ted had collected with other documents when he picked up the car. She remembered now he had pulled the MOT certificate from it on the first day to allay her fears about the accident to the car before they bought it. And there were the names. It was quite incredible the peace of mind they gave her. All her fears disappeared now that she was able to put a name to the man who had a family of two girls and a boy and a dog with a rough tongue. She knew she was right since Ted hadn't said any children were in the car crash, only a man and a woman.

There it was, 1st Owner; James Sutcliffe, 4, The Close, Salisbury. He had had the car for five years, it seemed, when the 2nd owner, took possession; Henry Oliver, 2 Maybrick Villas, Surbiton. She let the book fall to her lap, imagining the Sutcliffe family, their children and their dog. They were very close to her. Well, they sounded nice. And it was only when she saw that the 3rd owner was Tex Baxter that she realised.

'So that's who you were,' she said, 'Henry Oliver, Mr Incubus with a beard. You'll never frighten me again.' She closed the book and put the documents back in the glove compartment. She ran across the sand with her picnic basket in the direction of the old fish cellars. When Ted joined her she was leaning against the warm rocks, half asleep.

'I'm famished,' he said, drying himself. A couple were, now, walking across the sand at the water's edge. 'Come on, I want some coffee and cake or something. It's time for elevenses, anyway.'

'Henry Oliver,' she murmured softly, looking up at his naked body, admiring the strength of it.

'What the hell has he to do with anything? He's dead.'

She sat up with a jolt. 'He was the last owner of our car.'

'I know. He and his girl friend, or maybe his wife, were killed in that accident I told you about. In Rampart Street, Salisbury. Garage man told me. Thought it might put me off. I told him it didn't worry me. I mean you'd never buy anything, say a house for instance, if you were scared by people dying in it, would you?'

'But, but ...' she stammered.

'Well?'

'I bet you he had a beard and his girl had golden hair. Like that couple making love you thought you saw on our first night.'

Ted lay down in the sun, his body already the colour of

sand. 'God, Meg, you do think 'em up. How the hell can you possibly know that?'

'I don't really, but I'm pretty sure it was the first owner of the car who had a family and dog, the Sutcliffes, and a wife called Angela. They sound as if they did. You can laugh but I bet I'm right.' A further idea was milling round her mind. It had to be so; that grassy place they parked the car the first day of their arrival, her fright in the car and Ted finding the only pub in the little village so close. 'And what's more I'll prove it when we get back to supper.'

And there, in the pub's Visitor's Book, it was, only a year earlier. Henry Oliver, Mr and Mrs, 4, Maybrick Villas, Surbiton.

'You're a bloody miracle,' Ted said. 'You ought to have been a female detective not a librarian. I'll stand you a gin and tonic. You deserve it.'

Of course, she should have realised and made Ted take a different route. But the holiday had been so happy that she wanted it all over and them back in London as quickly as possible. She wanted to shut the album, as it were, on all the happiness, the sea, her early morning walks, the places they had driven to, the glory of the sunset over the immense headlands. She didn't want it fragmented; she wanted to hold it all in her hands, like a brilliant apple and say to herself, 'My Holiday.'

Now it was over and they were driving away only the good thing mattered, were to be remembered. And Henry Oliver, who had stayed in 'their' pub a year ago was now dead, poor fellow, had not been a good thing. Not if he and that 'bitch' could come back ... She shut the picture from her mind. To hell with him! After all it was their car now and, and ...

They left it as late as possible on Saturday, bathing and picnicing on their favourite beach until after three o'clock. The roads would be freer then, Ted said, and it didn't matter what time they arrived home, they'd have all Sunday to recover before going back to work.

They reached Salisbury after dark. The street lighting was on. They drove up Exeter Street and right into St Anne Street and then left to join the London Road. The road looked quite clear ahead and Ted accelerated. He swerved violently as the lorry bore down on them. Meg shouted and put her hands up to her face and tried to open the door.

'Get down,' Ted yelled, as the car hit the curb, too late and with too little space to manoeuvre out of the way of the lorry's cab. There was a fearful sound of breaking glass as it hit the side of the car, a tearing of brakes, and he was back in the deserted road, with only the street lights and shops ahead of him. The engine was still running. They were completely unharmed.

'It's all right, Meg, it's all right,' he kept on repeating in his shock, even though the car was shuddering under them, heaving and seeming ready to break apart. People were already running, passing their car to something behind them.

They were shocked, and Meg very white. She could hardly stand when she got out on to the pavement.

'Look,' Ted said, 'the car isn't even scratched. God knows what happened. I thought it hit us.'

But Meg had gone back. She was standing a little way from the huge lorry now embedded in a shop front. 'Oh, no, no,' she was crying when Ted reached her. 'It can't be, it can't.' A lane opened in the crowd which had mysteriously gathered and he saw, lying on the road, a man with a thin beard. Blood was trickling from his forehead, his body was squirming, half on, half off the pavement. Beside him, her head smashed like an egg, lay a young woman. All he seemed to recognize, as if in a dream, was her golden hair.

Ted understood the moment he took Meg into his arms and held her shaking body. Something was impelling him to look over her head at the sign above the last shop. RAMPART STREET, he read. He understood because the street was so silent, the crowd which had run to the scene of the accident made no noise at all. All you could see were their mouths opening and shutting, as if they were shouting. It was like looking at a TV set with the sound switched off.

A little later a police patrol car went slowly past them. The driver looked at him with Meg in his arms and then thought better of it. Two lovers just met in a deserted city street, nothing unusual in that, surely? Ted half raised his hand as if to summon them but he knew, now, a year after the accident happened, that it would be futile to call the police. They could not have seen what he and Meg were seeing. They would have thought him mad or drunk.

When he turned to look again at the dying and dead bodies of Henry Oliver and his 'wife', the street was quite empty but for their car standing by the curb, waiting for them.

III

No 1 Branch Line:
The Signalman
Charles Dickens

Charles Dickens (1812-70) wrote several short stories that have received less attention than his world-famous novels and this classic tale is one of them. This story was made into an excellent film and must surely be one of the first to feature the railway as a setting for a ghost story. Since then that mode of transport has received a great deal of attention and later variations are also included in this collection.

'Halloa! Below there!'

When he heard a voice thus calling to him, he was standing at the door of his box, with a flag in his hand, furled round its short pole. One would have thought, considering the nature of the ground, that he could not have doubted from what quarter the voice came; but instead of looking up to where I stood on the top of the steep cutting nearly over his head, he turned himself about, and looked down the line. There was something remarkable in his manner of doing so, though I could not have said for my life what. But I know it was remarkable enough to attract my notice, even though his figure was foreshortened and shadowed, down in the deep trench, and mine was high above him, so steeped in the glow of an angry sunset, that I had shaded my eyes with my hand before I saw him at all.

'Halloa! Below!'

From looking down the line, he turned himself about again and, raising his eyes, saw my figure high above him.

'Is there any path by which I can come down and speak to you?'

He looked up at me without replying, and I looked down at him without pressing him too soon with a repetition of my idle question. Just then there came a vague vibration in the earth and air, quickly changing into a violent pulsation, and an oncoming rush, that caused me to start back, as though it had force to draw me down. When such vapour as rose to my height from this rapid train had passed me, and was skimming away over the landscape, I looked down again, and saw him refurling the flag he had shown while the train went by.

I repeated my inquiry. After a pause, during which he seemed to regard me with fixed attention, he motioned with his rolled-up flag towards a point on my level, some two or three hundred yards distant. I called down to him, 'All right!' and made for that point. There, by dint of looking closely about me, I found a rough zigzag descending path notched out, which I followed.

The cutting was extremely deep, and unusually precipitate. It was made through a clammy stone, that became oozier and wetter as I went down. For these reasons, I found the way long enough to give me time to recall a singular air of reluctance or compulsion with which he had pointed out the path.

When I came down low enough upon the zigzag descent to see him again, I saw that he was standing between the rails on the way by which the train had lately passed, in an attitude as if he were waiting for me to appear. He had his left hand at his chin, and that left elbow rested on his right hand, crossed over his breast. His attitude was one of such expectation and watchfulness that I stopped a moment, wondering at it.

I resumed my downward way, and stepping out upon the level of the railroad, and drawing nearer to him, saw that he was a dark sallow man with a dark beard and rather heavy eyebrows. His post was in as solitary and dismal a place as ever I saw. On either side, a dripping-wet wall of jagged stone, excluding all view but a strip of sky; the perspective one way only a crooked prolongation of this great dungeon; the shorter perspective in the other direction terminating in a gloomy red light, and the gloomier entrance to a black tunnel, in whose massive architecture there was a barbarous, depressing, and forbidding air. So little sunlight ever found its way to this spot, that it had an earthy, deadly smell; and so much cold wind rushed through it, that it struck chill to me, as if I had left the natural world.

Before he stirred, I was near enough to him to have touched him. Not even then removing his eyes from mine, he stepped back one step, and lifted his hand.

This was a lonesome post to occupy (I said), and it had riveted my attention when I looked down from up yonder. A visitor was a rarity, I should suppose; not an unwelcome rarity, I hoped? In me, he merely saw a man who had been shut up within narrow limits all his life, and who, being at last set free, had a newly-awakened interest in these great works. To such purpose I spoke to him; but I am far from sure of the terms I used; for, besides that I am not happy in opening any conversation, there was something in the man that daunted me.

He directed a most curious look towards the red light near the tunnel's mouth, and looked all about it, as if something were missing from it, and then looked at me.

That light was part of his charge? Was it not?

He answered in a low voice – 'Don't you know it is?'

The monstrous thought came into my mind, as I perused the fixed eyes and the saturnine face, that this was a spirit, not a man. I have speculated since, whether there may have been infection in his mind.

In my turn I stepped back. But in making the action, I detected in his eyes some latent fear of me. This put the monstrous thought to flight.

'You look at me,' I said, forcing a smile, 'as if you had a dread of me.'

'I was doubtful,' he returned, 'whether I had seen you before.'

'Where?'

He pointed to the red light he had looked at.

'There?' I said.

Intently watchful of me, he replied (but without sound), 'Yes.'

'My good fellow, what should I do there? However, be that as it may, I never was there, you may swear.'

'I think I may,' he rejoined. 'Yes; I am sure I may.'

His manner cleared, like my own. He replied to my remarks with readiness, and in well-chosen words. Had he much to do there? Yes; that was to say, he had enough responsibility to bear; but exactness and watchfulness were what was required to him, and of actual work – manual labour – he had next to none. To change that signal, to trim those lights, and to turn this iron handle now and then, was all he had to do under that head. Regarding those many long and lonely hours of which I seemed to make so much, he could only say that the routine of his life had shaped itself into that form, and he had grown used to it. He had taught himself a language down here – if only to know it by sight, and to have formed his own crude ideas of its pronunciation, could be called learning it. He had also worked at fractions and decimals, and tried a little algebra; but he was, and had been as a boy, a poor hand at figures. Was it necessary for him when on duty always to remain in that channel of damp air, and could he never rise into the sunshine from between those high stone walls? Why, that depended upon time and circumstances. Under some conditions there would be less upon the line than under others, and the same held good as to certain hours of the day and night. In bright weather, he did choose occasions for getting a little above these lower shadows; but, being at all times liable to be called by his electric bell, and at such times listening for it with redoubled anxiety, the relief was less than I would suppose.

He took me into his box, where there was a fire, a desk for an official book in which he had to make certain entries, a telegraphic instrument with its dial, face and needles, and the little bell of which he had spoken. On my trusting that he would excuse the remark that he had been well educated, and (I hoped I might say without offence), perhaps educated above that station, he observed that instances of slight incongruity in such wise would rarely be found wanting among large bodies of men; that he had heard it was so in workhouses, in the police force, even in that last desperate resource, the army; and that he knew it was so, more or less, in any great railway staff. He had been, when young (if I could believe it, sitting in that hut – he scarcely could), a student of natural philosophy, and had attended lectures; but he had run wild, misused his opportunities, gone down, and never risen again. He had no complaint to offer about that. He had made his bed, and he lay upon it. It was far too late to make another.

All that I have here condensed he said in a quiet manner, with his grave dark regards divided between me and the fire. He threw in the word, 'Sir,' from time to time, and especially when he referred to his youth – as though to request me to understand that he claimed to be nothing but what I found him. He was several times interrupted by the little bell, and had to read off messages, and send replies. Once he had to stand without the door, and display a flag as a train passed, and make some verbal communication to the driver. In the discharge of his duties, I observed him to be remarkably exact and vigilant, breaking off his discourse at a syllable and remaining silent until what he had to do was done.

In a word, I should have set this man down as one of the safest of men to be employed in that capacity, but for the circumstances that while he was speaking to me he twice broke off with a fallen colour, turned his face towards the little bell when it did *not* ring, opened the door of the hut (which was kept shut to exclude the unhealthy damp), and looked out towards the red light near the mouth of the tunnel. On both of those occasions, he came back to the fire with the inexplicable air upon him which I had remarked, without being able to define, when we were so far asunder.

Said I, when I rose to leave him, 'You almost make me think that I have met with a contented man.'

(I am afraid I must acknowledge that I said it to lead him on.)

'I believe I used to be so,' he rejoined, in the low voice in which he had first spoken, 'but I am troubled, sir, I am troubled.'

He would have recalled the words if he could. He had said them, however, and I took them up quickly.

'With what? What is your trouble?'

'It is very difficult to impart, sir. It is very very difficult to speak of. If ever you make me another visit, I will try to tell you.'

'But I expressly intend to make you another visit. Say, when shall it be?'

'I go off early in the morning, and I shall be on again at ten tomorrow night, sir.'

'I will come at eleven.'

He thanked me, and went out at the door with me. 'I'll show my white light, sir,' he said, in his peculiar low voice, ''till you have found the way up. When you have found it, don't call out! And when you are at the top, don't call out.'

His manner seemed to make the place strike colder to me, but I said no more than, 'Very well.'

'And when you come down tomorrow night, don't call out! Let me ask you a parting question. What made you cry, "Halloa! Below there!" tonight?'

'Heaven knows,' said I, 'I cried something to that effect – '

'Not to that effect, sir. Those were the very words. I know them well.'

'Admit those were the very words. I said them, no doubt, because I saw you below.'

'For no other reason?'

'What other reason could I possibly have?'

'You had no feeling that they were conveyed to you in any supernatural way?'

'No.'

He wished me goodnight, and held up his light. I walked by the side of the down line of rails (with a very disagreeable sensation of a train coming behind me) until I found the path. It was easier to mount than to descend, and I got back to my inn without any adventure.

Punctual to my appointment, I placed my foot on the first notch of the zigzag next night, as the distant clocks were striking eleven. He was waiting for me at the bottom, with his white light on. 'I have not called out,' I said, when we came close together; 'may I speak now?' 'By all means, sir,' 'Goodnight, then, and here's my hand.' 'Goodnight, sir, and here's mine.' With that we walked side by side to his box, entered it, closed the door, and sat down by the fire.

'I have made up my mind, sir,' he began, bending forward as soon as we were seated, and speaking in a tone but a little above a whisper, 'that you shall not have to ask me twice what troubles me. I took you for someone else yesterday evening. That troubles me.'

'That mistake?'

'No. That was someone else.'

'Who is it?'

'I don't know.'

'Like me?'

'I don't know. I never saw the face. The left arm is across the face, and the right arm is waved – violently waved. This way.'

I followed his action with my eyes, and it was the action of an arm gesticulating, with the utmost passion and vehemence, 'For God's sake, clear the way!'

'One moonlight night,' said the man, 'I was sitting here, when I heard a voice cry, "Halloa! Below there!" I started up, looked from that door, and saw this Someone else standing by the red light near the tunnel, waving as I just now showed you. The voice seemed hoarse with shouting, and it cried, "Look out! Look out!" And then again, "Halloa! Below there! Look out!" I caught up my lamp, turned it on red, and ran towards the figure calling, "What's wrong? What has happened? Where?" It stood just outside the blackness of the tunnel. I advanced so close upon it that I wondered at its keeping the sleeve across its eyes. I ran right up at it, and had my hand stretched out to pull the sleeve away, when it was gone.'

'Into the tunnel?' said I.

'No. I ran on into the tunnel, five hundred yards. I stopped, and held my lamp above my head, and saw the figures of the measured distance, and saw the wet stains stealing down the walls and trickling through the arch. I ran out again faster than I had run in (for I had a mortal abhorrence of the place upon me), and I looked all round the red light with my own red light, and I went up the iron ladder to the gallery atop of it, and I came down again, and ran back here. I telegraphed both ways. "An alarm has been given. Is anything wrong?" The answer came back, both ways, "All well." '

Resisting the slow touch of a frozen finger tracing out my spine, I showed him how that this figure must be a deception of his sense of sight; and now that figures, originating in disease of the delicate nerves that minister to the functions of the eye, were known to have often troubled patients, some of whom had become conscious of the nature of their affliction, and had even proved it by experiments upon themselves. 'As to an imaginary cry,' said I, 'do but listen for a moment to the wind in this unnatural valley while we speak so low, and to the wild harp it makes of the telegraph wires.'

That was all very well, he returned, after we had sat listening for a while, and he ought to know something of the wind and the wires – he who so often passed long winter nights there, alone and watching. But he would beg to remark that he had not finished.

I asked his pardon, and he slowly added these words, touching my arm –

'Within six hours after the Appearance, the memorable accident on this line happened, and within ten hours the dead and wounded were brought along through the tunnel over the spot where the figure had stood.'

A disagreeable shudder crept over me, but I did my best against it. It was not to be denied, I rejoined, that this was a remarkable coincidence, calculated deeply to impress his mind. But it was unquestionable that remarkable coincidences did continually occur, and they must be taken into account in dealing with such a subject. Though to be sure I must admit, I added (for I thought I saw that he was going to bring the objection to bear upon me), men of common sense did not allow much for coincidences in making the ordinary calculations of life.

He again begged to remark that he had not finished.

I again begged his pardon for being betrayed into interruptions.

'This,' he said, again laying his hand upon my arm, and glancing over his shoulder with hollow eyes, 'was just a year ago. Six or seven months passed, and I had recovered from the surprise and shock, when one morning, as the day was breaking, I, standing at the door, looked towards the red light, and saw the spectre again.' He stopped with a fixed look at me.

'Did it cry out?'

'No, it was silent.'

'Did it wave its arm?'

'No. It leaned against the shaft of the light, with both hands before the face. Like this.'

Once more I followed his action with my eyes. It was an action of mourning. I have seen such an attitude on stone figures on tombs.

'Did you go up to it?'

'I came in and sat down, partly to collect my thoughts, partly because it had turned me faint. When I went to the door again, daylight was above me, and the ghost was gone.'

'But nothing followed? Nothing came of this?'

He touched me on the arm with his forefinger twice or thrice, giving a ghastly nod each time –

'That very day, as a train came out of the tunnel I noticed, at a carriage window on my side, what looked like a confusion of hands and heads, and something waved. I saw it just in time to signal the driver, Stop! He shut off, and put his brake on, but the train drifted past here a hundred and fifty yards or more. I ran after it, and, as I went along, heard terrible screams and cries. A beautiful young lady had died instantaneously in one of the compartments, and was brought in here, and laid down on this floor between us.'

Involuntarily I pushed my chair back, as I looked from the boards at which he pointed to himself.

'True, sir. True. Precisely as it happened, so I tell it you.'

I could think of nothing to say, to any purpose, and my mouth was very dry. The wind and the wires took up the story with a long lamenting wail.

He resumed, 'Now, sir, mark this, and judge how my mind is troubled. The spectre came back a week ago. Ever since, it has been there, now and again, by fits and starts.'

'At the light?'

'At the Danger-light.'

'What does it seem to do?'

He repeated, if possible with increased passion and vehemence, that former gesticulation of 'For God's sake, clear the way!'

Then he went on. 'I have no peace or rest for it. It calls to me, for many minutes together, in an agonized manner, "Below there! Look out! Look out!" It stands waving to me. It rings my little bell – '

I caught at that. 'Did it ring your bell yesterday evening when I was here, and you went to the door?'

'Twice.'

'Why, see,' said I, 'how your imagination misleads you. My eyes were on the bell, and my ears were open to the bell, and if

I am a living man, it did *not* ring at those times. No, nor at any other time, except when it was rung in the natural course of physical things by the station communicating with you.'

He shook his head. 'I have never made a mistake as to that yet, sir. I have never confused the spectre's ring with the man's. The ghost's ring is a strange vibration in the bell that it derives from nothing else, and I have not asserted that the bell stirs to the eye. I don't wonder that you failed to hear it. But *I* heard it.'

'And did the spectre seem to be there when you looked out?'

'It *was* there.'

'Both times?'

He repeated firmly, 'Both times.'

'Will you come to the door with me, and look for it now?'

He bit his under lip as though he were somewhat unwilling, but arose. I opened the door, and stood on the step, while he stood in the doorway. There was the danger-light. There was the dismal mouth of the tunnel. There were the high, wet stone walls of the cutting. There were the stars above them.

'Do you see it?' I asked him, taking particular note of his face. His eyes were prominent and strained, but not very much more so, perhaps, than my own had been when I had directed them earnestly towards the same spot.

'No,' he answered. 'It is not there.'

'Agreed,' said I.

We went in again, shut the door, and resumed our seats. I was thinking how best to improve this advantage, if it might be called one, when he took up the conversation in such a matter-of-course way, so assuming that there could be no serious question of fact between us, that I felt myself placed in the weakest of positions.

'By this time you will fully understand, sir,' he said, 'that what troubles me so dreadfully is the question, What does the spectre mean?'

I was not sure, I told him, that I did fully understand.

'What is its warning against?' he said, ruminating, with his eyes on the fire, and only by times turning them on me. 'What is the danger? Where is the danger? There is danger overhanging somewhere on the line. Some dreadful calamity will happen. It is not to be doubted this third time, after what has gone before. But surely this is a cruel haunting of *me*. What can I do?'

He pulled out his handkerchief, and wiped the drops from his heated forehead.

'If I telegraph Danger, on either side of me, or on both, I can give no reason for it,' he went on, wiping the palms of his hands. 'I should get into trouble and do no good. They would think I was mad. This is the way it would work – Message: "Danger! Take Care!" Answer: "What Danger? Where?" Message: "Don't know. But, for God's sake, take care!" They would displace me. What else could they do?'

His pain of mind was most pitiable to see. It was the mental torture of a conscientious man, oppressed beyond endurance by an unintelligible responsibility involving life.

'When it first stood under the Danger-light,' he went on, putting his dark hair back from his head, and drawing his hands outward across and across his temples in an extremity of feverish distress, 'why not tell me where that accident was to happen – if it must happen? Why not tell me how it could be averted – if it could have been averted? When on its second coming it hid its face, why not tell me, instead, "She is going to die. Let them keep her at home?" If it came, on those two occasions, only to show me that its warnings were true, and so to prepare me for the third, why not warn me plainly now? And I, Lord help me! A mere poor signalman on this solitary station! Why not go to somebody with credit to be believed, and power to act?'

When I saw him in this state, I saw that for the poor man's sake, as well as for the public safety, what I had to do for the time was to compose his mind. Therefore, setting aside all question of reality or unreality between us, I represented to him that whoever thoroughly discharged his duty must do well, and that at least it was his comfort that he understood his duty, though he did not understand these confounding Appearances. In this effort I succeeded far better than in the attempt to reason him out of his conviction. He became calm; the occupations incidental to his post as the night advanced began to make larger demands on his attention: and I left him at two in the morning. I had offered to stay through the night, but he would not hear of it.

That I more than once looked back at the red light as I ascended the pathway, that I did not like the red light, and that I should have slept but poorly if my bed had been under it, I see no reason to conceal. Nor did I like the two sequences of the accident and the dead girl. I see no reason to conceal that either.

But what ran most in my thoughts was the consideration how ought I to act, having become the recipient of this disclosure? I had proved the man to be intelligent, vigilant, painstaking, and exact; but how long must he remain so, in his state of mind? Though in a subordinate position still he held a most important trust, and would I (for instance) like to stake my life on the chance of his continuing to execute it with precision?

Unable to overcome a feeling that there would be something treacherous in my communicating what he had told me to his superiors in the Company, without first being plain with himself and proposing a middle course to him, I ultimately resolved to offer to accompany him (otherwise keeping his secret for the present) to the wisest medical practitioner we could hear of in those parts, and to take his opinion. A change in his time of duty would come round next night, he had apprized me, and he would be off an hour or two after sunrise, and on again soon after sunset. I had appointed to return accordingly.

Next evening was a lovely evening and I walked out early to enjoy it. The sun was not yet quite down when I traversed the field-path near the top of the deep cutting. I would extend my walk for an hour, I said to myself, half an hour on and half an hour back, and it would then be time to go to my signalman's box.

Before pursuing my stroll, I stepped to the brink and mechanically looked down, from the point from which I had first seen him. I cannot describe the thrill that seized upon me, when, close at the mouth of the tunnel, I saw the appearance of a man, with his left sleeve across his eyes, passionately waving his right arm.

The nameless horror that oppressed me passed in a moment, for in a moment I saw that this appearance of a man was a man indeed, and that there was a little group of other men, standing at a short distance, to whom he seemed to be rehearsing the gesture he made. The Danger-light was not yet lighted. Against its shaft a little low hut, entirely new to me, had been made of some wooden supports and tarpaulin. It looked no bigger than a bed.

With an irresistible sense that something was wrong – with a flashing self-reproachful fear that fatal mischief had come of my leaving the man there, and causing no one to be sent to overlook or correct what he did – I descended the notched path with all the speed I could make.

'What is the matter?' I asked the men.

'Signalman killed this morning, sir.'

'Not the man belonging to that box?'

'Yes, sir.'

'Not the man I know?'

'You will recognize him, sir, if you knew him,' said the man who spoke for the others, solemnly uncovering his own head, and raising an end of the tarpaulin, 'for his face is quite composed.'

'O, how did this happen, how did this happen?' I asked, turning from one to another as the hut closed in again.

'He was cut down by an engine, sir. No man in England knew his work better. But somehow he was not clear of the outer rail. It was just at broad day. He had struck the light, and had the lamp in his hand. As the engine came out of the tunnel, his back was towards her, and she cut him down. That man drove her, and was showing how it happened. Show the gentleman, Tom.'

The man who wore a rough dark dress, stepped back to his former place at the mouth of the tunnel.

'Coming round the curve of the tunnel, sir,' he said, 'I saw him at the end, like as if I saw him down a perspective-glass. There was no time to check speed, and I knew him to be very careful. As he didn't seem to take heed of the whistle, I shut it off when we were running down upon him, and called to him as loud as I could call.'

'What did you say?'

'I said, "Below there! Look out! Look out! For God's sake, clear the way!"'

I started.

'Ah! it was a dreadful time, sir. I never left off calling to him. I put my arm before my eyes not to see, and I waved this arm to the last; but it was no use.'

Without prolonging the narrative to dwell on any one of its curious circumstances more than on any other, I may, in closing it, point out the coincidence that the warning of the engine-driver included not only the words which the unfortunate Signalman had repeated to me as haunting him, but also the words which I myself – not he – had attached, and that only in my own mind, to the gesticulation he had imitated.

IV

No Ticket
Mary Williams

As Dr Beeching, Lord High Executioner of the railways, has left but a shadow of the former comprehensive network of lines linking the smallest hamlet with the largest city, the average person with insufficient funds to finance a car now has less opportunity to travel around his homeland in 1979 than Sherlock Holmes had with his indispensable Bradshaw a century before! This is known as progress, and means that outside the main inter-city areas and beyond the London commuter belt most rural communities if not entirely isolated are dependent on very sparse (and over-priced) bus routes. In Norfolk, Yorkshire and other remote places this means inconvenience, in the Cornwall of Mary Williams it can mean rather more ...

Mary Williams is now well-known for her collections of ghost stories. She lives in St Ives, and Cornwall is the setting and inspiration for many of them. As you will see, it is not always the land that the holidaymaker knows.

The mist was quickly thickening into fog, and I wondered why I hadn't had the sense to stop at the last village and put up for the night. But before starting off on my Cornish walking trip the doctor had said, 'Whatever you do get out into the fresh air and walk. Walk yourself so tired your body will fall to sleep the moment you get to bed. It's the only way, Rogers. Breakdowns are funny things. Drugs can help at the beginning, but in the end it's only nature and commonsense will do the trick. You're a fit enough man physically. So give the brain a bit of a rest, and you'll soon find the nightmares will go.'

Naturally I'd taken his advice, and for the first week things had gone better for me than I'd expected. It was autumn, with the moors washed bronze and gold under the pale sun, and the mingled smell of fallen leaves, blackberries and distant tang of woodsmoke hovering rich in the air with the faint drift of sea-blown brine. Heady, nostalgic weather, stirring the lost emotion of youth to life again. Not difficult then to push the rat-race of London journalism behind me, forgetting even ... except in sudden rare stabs of renewed pain ... my break with Clare.

Each day I'd walked a little further, and when I came to some attractive looking old inn catering for visitors had stopped for the night, setting off again after a hearty breakfast for further exercise and adventure.

Yes, there was adventure in the experience; mostly I suppose because of the terrain ... Cornwall. Changeless in the sense of atmosphere and 'place' magic, yet at almost every corner providing a vista of alternating scene. At one moment lush and verdant between high hedges and clumps of woodland, the next opening to stretches of barren countryside dotted with the stark relics of ruined mine works and huddled granite hamlets perched above the windblown cliffs. As I trod the winding lanes and moorland roads of West Penwith this sense of agelessness and primitive challenge had deepened and drawn me on, almost as though into another dimension.

I should have stopped at The Tramping Woman of course, an ancient hostelry on the outskirts of Wikka; but ignored it and continued along the high road between coast and rocky hills, although the sun was already dying, leaving a film of pale gold beneath the greenish sky.

I'd walked almost a mile to the west when the mist started to rise; thinly at first, like a gauze veil over the fading landscape, then thickening into furry uncertainty so the boulders and windblown trees assumed gradually the menacing quality of ancient gigantic beasts and legendary creatures risen to torment and mislead. When I came at last to a crossroads with a decrepit sign-post pointing in three directions like a gibbet, I paused searching for my torch to try and locate any names given. It was impossible. The archaic lettering further distorted by the wreathing fog made no sense at all. In fact as I went close up, clinging to the post, the cloying atmosphere completely shrouded it into negation, warning me that far from improving, the light and weather were steadily getting worse.

A sickening sense of claustrophobia filled me, choking at my throat, filling my lungs with a hysterical feeling of being unable to breathe. The torch suddenly flickered and went out. I was alone, and lost, and if I hadn't forced myself to move quickly I knew I'd be there until morning, by which time, for me, it might be too late.

So I struck ahead taking what I thought ... or hoped ... was the main road.

How long I continued in this way, moving by instinct rather than any coherent sense of direction I don't know. Occasionally I lurched against a bush or humped tree ... maybe something more sinister ... that flapped me with the clammy slap of a dead hand. Once I fell against a looming slab of stone that emitted to my distorted fancy malicious elemental glee as I pulled myself away with my heart pumping furiously. I could imagine the ancient cromlechs and standing stones on the moors above leering down on my puny shape as I struggled blindly on, with my coat gripped close over my chest, head thrust forward in a futile attempt to get a clear glimpse of the ground.

Except for the dripping of the fog, the stillness was oppressive ... an entity in itself. Watchfulness encompassed me. From the furry grey walls on every side it seemed to me that eyes were peering. Secret haunted eyes of elemental evil and atavistic greed. Unconsciously I put out an arm to defend myself, knowing that I couldn't continue for much longer. My thighs already felt deadened, the breath in my body absorbed by the sucking lips and tongue of hungry fog.

And then, suddenly, I heard it; the distant thrum of an engine ... tangible evidence of reality in an unreal world. A car or bus surely? 'Thank God,' I thought, swerving to the side of the road.

A minute later headlights appeared dimly, emerging as two immense wan eyes through the curdling fitful grey. The road temporarily came into blurred focus ... snaking like some ghostly ribbon towards me until the cumbrous dark shape dimmed it again into darkness. The vehicle seemed to sway slightly and slow down as it passed; sufficiently for me to pull myself by the rail over the step inside.

I paused briefly, gasping for breath, then staggered on flinging myself into the first vacant seat. Only one dim light shone from the front, showing the dark shoulders of the driver at the wheel and above, in the vicinity of the windscreen, the glow of a printed name, ABMUT, which was a new one on me. I'd never heard of the place, and never been in such an antiquated omnibus before. It was a real 'bone-shaker', and as we jogged on, with the dripping fog flapping the windscreen, streaming in rivulets down the dreary windows, I could almost hear my own jaws and knees creaking in unison with the macabre tempo of the ancient engine.

There were about a dozen passengers inside, no more, and they were a silent crowd, sitting speechless and hunched into their grey clothes, faces pale discs of misery, eyes mere shadowed pools of emptiness in the queer half light. My presence seemed to evoke no interest whatever, the entrance of a stranger generally does on a country journey.

Thinking back now, I can't recall a single individual face except those of an aged bearded man with a kind of muffler round his head, a lantern-jawed woman wearing a grey hooded cape, and a young boy who seemed more alert than the rest, although his forehead was bandaged, and I guessed he'd been in an accident. He looked round once at me, and I saw in his eyes such supplication and pleading I hoisted myself up and went to sit beside him. No one seemed to notice. There was no comment, no flicker of surprise or movement from the crouched chill forms. Even the child himself didn't speak; but I could feel him shivering, and when my hand touched his it was icily cold. But I felt he was grateful to have me there.

How long that dreary journey to Abmut took, I've no idea. Time seemed to have died. The silence, except for the monotonous chug-chugging of the engine, was oppressive and somehow unearthly. There were only brief intervals when the landscape took form, showing a momentary glimpse of a looming hill-side or humped boulder at a corner of the lane. Still, I thought, Abmut must be our destination, and where there was a village or town, presumably there would be an inn, however primitive. I had a compulsive almost irrational desire at one point to get up and jump out. But as I made the first instinctive movement, several heads turned to look at me, and their dumb, pale, almost hostile faces filled me with such aversion I remained rooted to the spot, my hand automatically tightening on the boy's.

If there'd been a conductor I'd have forced information from him, but the vehicle was obviously a one-man affair as some still are in remote places; therefore all I could do was to hope for the best, and somehow battle against the sickening fear which was intensifying in me every moment that passed.

At last through the window I saw thankfully the first glimmer of lifting light in a fold of the moors below the road. As the bus took a sharp turn down a steep track between dripping walls of hedges, the blurred outline of a huddled hamlet took shape, dimly at first ... a mere outline of grey squat buildings that gradually clarified, assuming a quivering brilliance against that desolate landscape of grim uniformity. It was as though nature, in a quixotic moment had designed a macabre backcloth purely as a setting for this one benighted village.

And then the singing began ... from a church presumably ... although the soughing and sighing and rising and falling of the mournful yet unwelcoming chorus held, for my ears, more of the wind's moan and the sea's lonely call than the quality of human voices. At the same time I was aware of movement, a shuffling and stirring around me as one form after another moved cumbrously from each seat and waited, heads hunched forward, for the bus to stop.

It came to a halt at the top of a track about a hundred yards from the hamlet which appeared by then to emerge from a sea of vaporised grey, roof tops and church spire tipped with silver. I waited until the last of the throng, the boy, had clambered out. The driver had dismounted and was waiting to give a nod before each joined the mournful procession downwards. Then I swung myself wearily by the rail to the ground.

'Ticket?' I heard him murmur above the weird cacophony of sighs that rose and fell intermittently on a drift of rising wind. His voice was hushed yet grating, like the branch of a very ancient tree about to snap, the dark holed eyes watchful from the bearded face. Drifts of grey hair blew fitfully in the clammy air, brushing my face softly with the choking touch of a cobwebbed shroud.

Revolted, I drew away.

'I've no ticket,' I told him.

'No ticket?' He shook his head as the mist curdled and cleared again briefly, revealing a mournful dropped jaw and skeleton-like visage moving incredulously on a thin neck.

'That's right,' I said, 'I got on further back, where you slowed down? I can pay now, and the rest necessary to take me on. Or ... are you returning to Wikka?' As I spoke the wild hope stirred in me this might be so. I had a growing irrational desire to be away from Abmut as soon as possible. In spite of the gathering radiance there and the muted singing which was gradually dying into a subdued murmur, there was something odd and greedy about the place ... something sensed rather than seen that appalled me.

Then he spoke in a wheezing voice that was more of a harsh whisper, holding condemnation in it as well as a threat.

'There's no return from here. No one leaves once they've come. *No* one ...'

A crawling shuddering fear pricked my spine. I could feel my nails digging into my palms. What do you mean no one leaves? What the hell *is* this place ... this *Abmut*?'

Before the mist clouded his face into a mere blurred disc I saw the lips stretch in an obscene grin from ear to ear. 'Not Abmut,' he muttered in the same sibilant undertone. 'Tumba. That's the name. Tumba.' And the laughter rose from his ancient throat more harsh than the sound of dried bones cracking on stone, colder and more deadly than death itself.

Forcing myself to mobility I rushed, half staggering, to the front of the bus. It was just as he said ... TUMBA printed at the top of the front window in stygian green lettering that for a moment caught all the reflected light from the hamlet below. What I'd seen from the inside had been the wrong way round.

TUMBA.

It took some moments for the truth to register, and when at last the meaning of the word penetrated my cold brain, I rushed as though in some nightmare of doom over the rim of the slope. From there, against the quivering uncertain vista of fog mingled with luminous quivering light, the sad, limping, column of shuffling figures was visible; grey humped forms moving rhythmically and with an inevitability of purpose that I knew no human hand could allay.

Shuddering, I watched helplessly, as for a brief space of time the fog lifted, under a green sky, revealing a gaunt landscape of tumbled rock and giant standing-stones where the hamlet had formerly been. All sound except the screaming of gulls and moaning of the strengthening wind had died. There was no singing any more, no murmur of voices or whispered comment from the macabre driver, and when I turned there was no sign of him at all. Nothing but dripping negation ... an emptiness and desolation so intense it seemed that no human foot had ever stepped there.

I looked again, towards the column of creeping shuffling beings, and as I stood watching, impelled by some dark power impossible to combat, the pale stones toppled and the earth opened with a shriek. Greedy grey arms clawed upwards through the brown earth, with skeleton fingers reaching for their own. Skulls leered and lolled among the stones, jaws bared in unholy welcome, the whole scene becoming a seething struggling vortex of death and decay ... a lustful avaricious breeding ground for the terrifying 'earth-bound' and the damned.

Sickened I had to wait while the crowd of erstwhile passengers suddenly lunged forward and were taken to their own corruption. The ground closed over them like an immense elemental mouth devouring, with a shudder, its own.

All but the boy.

When the heaving and roaring of the earth had subsided, I saw him lying there by a shining white stone. The mist had dispersed considerably, and nothing moved over that lonely terrain but a bird's sudden flight and squawking from the undergrowth. I looked behind me; the moorland road above the slope was almost clear; pale and empty under an eerie moonlit sky. No sign of any vehicle or indication there had ever been one.

Slowly I turned and made my way to where the recumbent young form lay stretched on his back in the heather. There was no fear on his face, for the innocent have no need of it;

only a tremendous loneliness and sadness for the days he should have had.

Automatically I crossed his hands over his chest and touched his cold forehead once, where the bandage had been torn away. The scar was vivid still from the impact that had taken his life. In that moment his delicate features were impressed indelibly and forever into my mind.

Just then I had neither the wish or strength to rationalise my haunting and macabre experience. It was all I could do to get to my feet, somehow making my way to the main moorland road.

Once there all initiative and sense of purpose faded into dark overwhelming negation. There was a roaring in my ears, a sound as though the universe was crumbling around me, and then I fell.

When I recovered consciousness I was aware only of greyness at first; a furry grey that slowly lifted to clean calm white. There was a face above me, a woman's face in a nurse's cap, and very gradually it dawned on me I was in hospital. My head was aching abominably, yet memory still registered with dreadful disconcerting clarity.

I think I said something about 'Tumba'. She merely smiled, took my wrist between finger and thumb, a thermometer in the other hand, and after a minute said quietly, 'You're doing fine, Mr Rogers. Rest now. The doctor will be in presently.'

'Who found me?' I asked. 'How could anyone know I was there, by that awful place?'

'The driver, of course,' she replied. 'There was an accident. You swerved in the fog ...'

'No, no,' I told her, as my heart started to pump rapidly against my ribs, 'there was no accident. I got on to a bus, a pretty nasty vehicle. And when it stopped we were at Tumba. It was ... *foul* ...'

'Shsh ...' she said, 'you mustn't excite yourself. Concussion plays strange tricks with the memory. In time everything will become normal again ...'

But it never did; not quite. Eventually I had to accept that I had been involved in some sort of a crash on that benighted moorland road. The driver of a perfectly ordinary car verified this in his statement to the police, and his word was accepted. Perhaps I might even have persuaded myself in the end there was nothing more to it, if something rather odd hadn't happened a few days later.

By then, having mostly recovered from physical cuts and shock, I was able to sit up in bed and glance at a local weekly newspaper.

At the middle page I got a start. There, facing me, was the smiling photograph of a boy. A face I well knew, of the youngster who'd ridden beside me on that ghastly bus bound for Tumba, and whose cold forehead I'd touched with my hand before making for the road again.

Beneath the heading of 'TRAFFIC ACCIDENT' I read:

Anthony Treneer, aged twelve, died yesterday when a car skidded in the fog across the moorland road above Wikka. He had been out walking with a friend and was returning to Verrys Farm, his home, when the tragedy occurred. Death was instantaneous. He was the younger son of Mr and Mrs Robert Treneer, both well known and respected members of the farming community.

I was still staring at the paragraph when my nurse entered.

'That's the boy,' I said, pointing to the photograph.

'You knew him?'

'He was on the bus with me,' I told her unthinkingly, 'the bus to Tumba.'

'Tumba?' she said half pityingly. 'You must forget all about that. It was just an illusion, a nightmare.'

Her obtuseness suddenly irritated me.

'That's what you always say I suppose when you come up against something that can't be rationally explained. The fact remains, nurse, I'm not out of my mind, and although the whole thing may appear moonshine to you, the boy was *with* me ...'

Her voice was clipped when she said, 'He can't have been. Your accident took place at least three miles from the spot where he was hit. Another thing ... there's no such place as Tumba, and there never has been. Now you really must try and put such morbid fancies behind you, Mr Rogers. Thinking that way won't help your complete recovery at all.'

Realising there was no point in further argument, I let the matter drop. Whether she realised the significance of the name 'Tumba' was doubtful. But in an ancient dictionary of mine it is alluded to as a *tomb*.

Incidentally, the evening of the boy's death was the same as that of my haunted 'bus' journey. The only difference being, I suppose, he had a ticket out of this life, whereas I had none.

V

John Charrington's Wedding
E. Nesbit

Edith Nesbit (1858-1924) is a popular choice for compilers of macabre tales and many of her short stories are superb specimens of the economy and style of a master. All of us make journeys that we don't particularly wish to but few of us fail to arrive on the most important date of our lives, our wedding day. Perhaps John Charrington's determination went rather further than usual however ...

No one ever thought that May Forster would marry John Charrington; but he thought differently, and things which John Charrington intended had a queer way of coming to pass. He asked her to marry him before he went up to Oxford. She laughed and refused him. He asked her again next time he came home. Again she laughed, tossed her dainty blonde head, and again refused. A third time he asked her; she said it was becoming a confirmed bad habit, and laughed at him more than ever.

John was not the only man who wanted to marry her: she was the belle of our village coterie, and we were all in love with her more or less; it was a sort of fashion, like heliotrope ties or Inverness capes. Therefore we were as much annoyed as surprised when John Charrington walked into our little local club – we held it in a loft over the saddler's, I remember – and invited us all to his wedding.

'Your wedding?'

'You don't mean it?'

'Who's the happy fair? When's it to be?'

John Charrington filled his pipe and lighted it before he replied. Then he said:

'I'm sorry to deprive you fellows of your only joke – but

Miss Forster and I are to be married in September.'

'You don't mean it?'

'He's got the mitten again, and it's turned his head.'

'No,' I said, rising, 'I see it's true. Lend me a pistol someone – or a first-class fare to the other end of Nowhere. Charrington has bewitched the only pretty girl in our twenty-mile radius. Was it mesmerism, or a love-potion, Jack?'

'Neither, sir, but a gift you'll never have – perseverance – and the best luck a man ever had in this world.'

There was something in his voice that silenced me, and all chaff of the other fellows failed to draw him further.

The queer thing about it was that when we congratulated Miss Forster, she blushed and smiled and dimpled, for all the world as though she were in love with him, and had been in love with him all the time. Upon my word, I think she had. Women are strange creatures.

We were all asked to the wedding. In Brixham everyone who was anybody knew everybody else who was any one. My sisters were, I truly believe, more interested in the trousseau than the bride herself, and I was to be best man. The coming marriage was much canvassed at afternoon tea-tables, and at our little club over the saddler's, and the question was always asked: 'Does she care for him?'

I used to ask that question myself in the early days of their engagement, but after a certain evening in August I never asked it again. I was coming home from the club through the churchyard. Our church is on a thyme-grown hill, and the turf about it is so thick and soft that one's footsteps are noiseless.

I made no sound as I vaulted the low lichened wall, and threaded my way between the tombstones. It was at the same instant that I heard John Charrington's voice, and saw Her. May was sitting on a low flat gravestone, her face turned towards the full splendour of the western sun. Its expression ended, at once and for ever, any question of love for him; it was transfigured to a beauty I should not have believed possible, even to that beautiful little face.

John lay at her feet, and it was his voice that broke the stillness of the golden August evening.

'My dear, my dear, I believe I should come back from the dead if you wanted me!'

I coughed at once to indicate my presence, and passed on into the shadow fully enlightened.

The wedding was to be early in September. Two days before I had to run up to town on business. The train was late, of course, for we are on the South-Eastern, and as I stood grumbling with my watch in my hand, whom should I see but John Charrington and May Forster. They were walking up and down the unfrequented end of the platform, arm in arm, looking into each other's eyes, careless of the sympathetic interest of the porters.

Of course I knew better than to hesitate a moment before burying myself in the booking-office, and it was not till the train drew up at the platform, that I obtrusively passed the pair with my Gladstone, and took the corner in a first-class smoking-carriage. I did this with as good an air of not seeing them as I could assume. I pride myself on my discretion, but if John were travelling alone I wanted his company. I had it.

'Hullo, old man,' came his cheery voice as he swung his bag into my carriage; 'here's luck, I was expecting a dull journey!'

'Where are you off to?' I asked, discretion still bidding me turn my eyes away, though I saw, without looking, that hers were red-rimmed.

'To old Branbridge's,' he answered, shutting the door and leaning out for a last word with his sweetheart.

'Oh, I wish you wouldn't go, John,' she was saying in a low earnest voice. 'I feel certain something will happen.'

'Do you think I should let anything happen to keep me, and the day after tomorrow our wedding-day?'

'Don't go,' she answered, with a pleading intensity which would have sent my Gladstone on to the platform and me after it. But she wasn't speaking to me. John Charrington was made differently; he rarely changed his opinions, never his resolutions.

He only stroked the little ungloved hands that lay on the carriage door.

'I must, May. The old boy's been awfully good to me, and now he's dying I must go and see him, but I shall come home in time for – ' the rest of the parting was lost in a whisper and in the rattling lurch of the starting train.

'You're sure to come?' she spoke as the train moved.

'Nothing shall keep me,' he answered; and we steamed out. After he had seen the last of the little figure on the platform he leaned back in his corner and kept silence for a minute.

When he spoke it was to explain to me that his godfather, whose heir he was, lay dying at Peasmarsh Place, some fifty miles away, and had sent for John, and John had felt bound to go.

'I shall be surely back tomorrow,' he said, 'or, if not, the day after, in heaps of time. Thank Heaven, one hasn't to get up in the middle of the night to get married nowadays!'

'And suppose Mr Branbridge dies?'

'Alive or dead I mean to be married on Thursday!' John answered, lighting a cigar and unfolding *The Times*.

At Peasmarsh station we said good-bye, and he got out, and I saw him ride off. I went on to London, where I stayed the night.

When I got home the next afternoon, a very wet one, by the way, my sister greeted me with:

'Where's Mr Charrington?'

'Goodness knows,' I answered testily. Every man, since Caine, has resented that kind of question.

'I thought you might have heard from him,' she went on, 'as you're to give him away tomorrow.'

'Isn't he back?' I asked, for I had confidently expected to find him at home.

'No, Geoffrey,' – my sister Fanny always had a way of jumping to conclusions, especially such conclusions as were least favourable to her fellow-creatures – 'he has not returned, and what is more, you may depend upon it he won't. You mark my words, there'll be no wedding tomorrow.'

My sister Fanny has a power of annoying me which no other human being possesses.

'You mark my words,' I retorted with asperity, 'you had better give up making such a thundering idiot of yourself. There'll be more wedding tomorrow than ever you'll take the first part in.' A prophecy which, by the way, came true.

But though I could snarl confidently to my sister, I did not feel so comfortable when late that night, I, standing on the doorstep of John's house, heard that he had not returned. I went home gloomily through the rain. Next morning brought a brilliant blue sky, gold sun, and all such softness of air and beauty of cloud as go to make up a perfect day. I woke with a vague feeling of having gone to bed anxious, and of being rather averse to facing that anxiety in the light of full wakefulness.

But with my shaving-water came a note from John which relieved my mind and sent me up to the Forster's with a light heart.

May was in the garden. I saw her blue gown through the hollyhocks as the lodge gates swung to behind me. So I did not go up to the house, but turned aside down the turfed path.

'He's written to you, too,' she said, without preliminary greeting, when I reached her side.

'Yes, I'm to meet him at the station at three, and come straight on to the church.'

Her face looked pale, but there was a brightness in her eyes, and a tender quiver about the mouth that spoke of renewed happiness.

'Mr Branbridge begged him so to stay another night that he had not the heart to refuse,' she went on. 'He is so kind, but I wish he hadn't stayed.'

I was at the station at half past two. I felt rather annoyed with John. It seemed a sort of slight to the beautiful girl who loved him, that he should come as it were out of breath, and with the dust of travel upon him, to take her hand, which some of us would have given the best years of our lives to take.

But when the three o'clock train glided in, and glided out again having brought no passengers to our little station, I was more than annoyed. There was no other train for thirty-five minutes; I calculated that, with much hurry, we might just get to the church in time for the ceremony; but, oh, what a fool to miss that first train! What other man could have done it?

That thirty-five minutes seemed a year, as I wandered round the station reading the advertisements and the time-tables, and the company's bye-laws, and getting more and more angry with John Charrington. This confidence in his own power of getting everything he wanted the minute he wanted it was leading him too far. I hate waiting. Everyone does, but I believe I hate it more than anyone else. The three thirty-five was late, of course.

I ground my pipe between my teeth and stamped with impatience as I watched the signals. Click. The signal went down. Five minutes later I flung myself into the carriage that I had brought for John.

'Drive to the church!' I said, as someone shut the door. 'Mr Charrington hasn't come by this train.'

Anxiety now replaced anger. What had become of the man? Could he have been taken suddenly ill? I had never known him have a day's illness in his life. And even so he might have telegraphed. Some awful accident must have happened to him. The thought that he had played her false never – no, not for a moment – entered my head. Yes, something terrible had happened to him, and on me lay the task of telling his bride. I almost wished the carriage would upset and break my head so that someone else might tell her, not I, who – but that's nothing to do with this story.

It was five minutes to four as we drew up at the churchyard gate. A double row of eager onlookers lined the path from lychgate to porch. I sprang from the carriage and passed up between them. Our gardener had a good front place near the door. I stopped.

'Are they waiting still, Byles?' I asked, simply to gain time, for of course I knew they were by the waiting crowd's attentive attitude.

'Waiting, sir? No, no, sir; why, it must be over by now.'

'Over! Then Mr Charrington's come?'

'To the minute, sir; must have missed you somehow, and I say, sir,' lowering his voice, 'I never see Mr John the least bit so afore, but my opinion is he's been drinking pretty free. His clothes was all dusty and his face like a sheet. I tell you I didn't like the looks of him at all, and the folks inside are saying all sorts of things. You'll see, something's gone very wrong with Mr John, and he's tried liquor. He looked like a ghost, and in he went with his eyes straight before him, with never a look or a word for none of us: him that was always such a gentleman!'

I had never heard Byles make so long a speech. The crowd in the churchyard were talking in whispers and getting ready rice and slippers to throw at the bride and bridegroom. The ringers were ready with their hands on the ropes to ring out the merry peal as the bride and bridegroom should come out.

A murmur from the church announced them; out they came, Byles was right. John Charrington did not look himself. There was dust on his coat, his hair was disarranged. He seemed to have been in some row, for there was a black mark above his eyebrow. He was deathly pale. But his pallor was not greater than that of the bride, who might have been carved in ivory – dress, veil, orange blossoms, face and all.

As they passed out the ringers stooped – there were six of them – and then, on the ears expecting the gay wedding peal, came the low tolling of the passing bell.

A thrill of horror at so foolish a jest from the ringers passed through us all. But the ringers themselves dropped the ropes and fled like rabbits out into the sunlight. The bride shuddered, and grey shadows came about her mouth, but the bridegroom led her on down the path where the people stood with the handfuls of rice; but the handfuls were never thrown, and the wedding-bells never rang. In vain the ringers were urged to remedy their mistake; they protested with many whispered expletives that they would see themselves further first.

In a hush like the hush in the chamber of death the bridal pair passed into their carriage and its door slammed behind them.

Then the tongues were loosed. A babel of anger, wonder, conjecture from the guests and the spectators.

'If I'd seen his condition, sir,' said old Forster to me as we drove off, 'I would have stretched him on the floor of the church, sir, by Heaven I would, before I'd have let him marry my daughter!'

Then he put his head out of the window.

'Drive like hell,' he cried to the coachman; 'don't spare the horses.'

He was obeyed. We passed the bride's carriage. I forbore to look at it, and old Forster turned his head away and swore. We reached home before it.

We stood in the hall doorway, in the blazing afternoon sun, and in about half a minute we heard wheels crunching the gravel. When the carriage stopped in front of the steps old Forster and I ran down.

'Great Heaven, the carriage is empty! And yet – '

I had the door open in a minute, and this is what I saw –

No sign of John Charrington; and of May, his wife, only a huddled heap of white satin lying half on the floor of the carriage and half on the seat.

'I drove straight here, sir,' said the coachman, as the bride's father lifted her out; 'and I'll swear no one got out of the carriage.'

We carried her into the house in her bridal dress and drew back her veil. I saw her face. Shall I ever forget it? White, white and drawn with agony and horror, bearing such a look of terror as I have never seen since except in dreams. And her hair, her radiant blonde hair, I tell you it was white like snow.

As we stood, her father and I, half mad with the horror and mystery of it, a boy came up the avenue – a telegraph boy. They brought the orange envelope to me. I tore it open.

MR CHARRINGTON WAS THROWN FROM THE DOGCART ON HIS WAY TO THE STATION AT HALF PAST ONE. KILLED ON THE SPOT!

And he was married to May Forster in our parish church at half past three, in presence of half the parish.

'I shall be married dead or alive!'

What had passed in that carriage on the homeward drive? No one knows – no one will ever know. Oh, May! oh, my dear!

Before a week was over they laid her beside her husband in our little churchyard on the thyme-covered hill – the churchyard where they had kept their love-trysts.

Thus was accomplished John Charrington's wedding.

VI

Silent Stowaway
Rick Ferreira

Originally from the West Indies, Rick Ferreira now lives in Hampstead, and is speedily making a name for himself in the field of the supernatural and the macabre. He has published a collection of his own stories, and edited another. He also writes for television, and for children. 'Silent Stowaway', he tells me, is based on an experience of his own some years ago.

Dr McPhee awoke to the steady rhythmic thump of the ship's engines and with an instant return of the contentment he had known the night before as he drifted into sleep, slightly cramped though he was in the narrow bunk. But slept well he had, in spite of a heavy frame that stopped just short of the six foot mark and so wasn't quite the build for bunk-sleeping. He lay for a moment lazily analysing smells and sounds, before making a sketchy gesture at stretching. The best thing about a small freighter, Dr McPhee thought, was the fact that one was always so physically near to smells: of diesel oil, fresh varnish and paint, food trailers from the galley, the distinct clean-wet smell of swabbed decks.

With a passage on a regular liner, all this would have been nicely distanced. Sheer size would have seen to that. Now, in his tiny cabin on the *Hollander*, ten hours out of Paramaribo, Surinam, a hint of oven heat was already blowing over Dr McPhee's face – tropical heat that he would miss in London, although it was high summer there. London – then on to his sister's rambling house at Herne Hill and the start of a six months' holiday, interrupted only by a proposed lecture at the School of Tropical Medicine.

Dr McPhee had run a Caribbean practice for an unbroken five year stint in Georgetown, British Guiana. There he had felt needed and year after year had refused to take a break and a boat to England. Until now. A severe attack of malaria fever had shown him that a doctor was as mortal as the next man. Now, he knew he was lucky to be alive, almost fully recovered, and en route for home ...

Dr McPhee finally did some muscle-flexing instead of his usual giant stretch, then he peered at the wristwatch he brought close to deep-set grey eyes. He could just see that it was six forty-five.

The slap and swish of water seemed to fill the cabin and somewhere below decks, one of the Dutch crew was whistling an unrecognisable tune. Less than half a day from land and already the world had shrunk to the dimensions of one small ship, with nothing but water, behind and ahead. Yet Dr McPhee was satisfied. He sat up cautiously but still managed to bang his head on the narrow shelf above the bunk. At that moment there was a small thump on the cabin door.

'Come in!' Dr McPhee rubbed his head and waited.

But no one did. Instead there was a small high squeal and another thump on his door, then uncertain, irregular feet were slapping flatly in the passage outside. A few seconds of silence then again the slap-slap of the erratic feet, ending again with another small thump on the cabin door. Dr McPhee swung himself out of the bunk and, without pausing to collect and put on his glasses, crossed to the door and opened it – and a small boy tumbled headlong into the cabin.

Dr McPhee was surprised and instantly amused. He liked children. And there was no mistaking the sex of the toddler; all the boy wore was a short white vest. He got back on his chubby feet then gazed upwards with two enormous dark eyes, set in a round face that was the colour of rich brown chocolate. His sudden smile revealed two white and tiny teeth and then the boy put his rounded arms high above his head, as if his balance depended on the act.

'And what can I do for you?' Dr McPhee asked, preparing to stoop to a more practical level. But the boy had turned, arms still above his head, and stamped back into the passage. Dr McPhee followed and from the door he watched as the boy, shrieking with laughter, headed straight for the door that opened on to the after-deck. But it was closed – and, leaning against it, a woman was standing guard.

Dr McPhee saw her clearly.

He saw her as clearly as he could see anything or anyone without his glasses. She stood very still as the boy charged down on her ... she stood against the high polish of the closed door, sunlight and water making endless ripples across the blue of her dress. The toddler was almost on her when he cried in a half shout: '*De moeder!*' A second later and the boy had banged himself flat against the closed door; then, shrieking with laughter, he headed unsteadily back towards Dr McPhee. Then the chubby feet did a sudden swerve and the boy turned and disappeared into the cabin on the right. It was only then that Dr McPhee noticed that the door had been ajar. It did not stay that way for long. Pushing from behind it, the toddler slammed the door shut with an almighty bang.

Dr McPhee came back into his cabin and stood for a long moment without moving. Then he crossed to the railed shelf to collect his glasses, sponge-bag and shaving-kit. If he hurried there was every chance he'd be the first to use one of the two showers reserved for passengers – and the water would be hot enough for a close shave. Next door, as he got into his dressing gown, he heard the boy laughing gleefully. The boy was still laughing when Dr McPhee collected the fresh towel from the rail by the bunk, and left his cabin.

Dr McPhee was soaping himself under the uncertain stream from the shower when the odd thing about the recent scene finally struck home. It caught him off-guard, like an unexpected blow ... The tall black girl in the blue dress who had stood so serenely on guard, hadn't she vanished before the toddler hit the door? Had he actually seen her – or hadn't he? Without his glasses and with the shifting sunlight bouncing off the sea –

Someone gave a sharp rap on the small cubicle and a voice said, 'Good morning. I'm next in line ...' Dr McPhee recognised the voice – broad Scots and sounding still thick of tongue from last night's drinking session. The Sinclair chap, one of the four sugar planters who were going home on their 'long leave'.

'Won't be a minute,' Dr McPhee called out and started towelling vigorously.

Dr McPhee made his way below deck to the dining saloon and the burly Dutchman whom he knew to be the Chief Purser, stepped aside as he climbed down. At the foot of the stairs the Purser smiled and said, '*Goeden morgen!*' Dr McPhee smiled back. 'Good morning! Oh, by the way ... we did take on passengers at Surinam, didn't we, Purser? That must have been after midnight. I turned in rather early ...'

'Passengers? Yes. You will meet later, I am sure.'

'Yes,' Dr McPhee said dryly, 'I've yet to meet the grown-ups!'

So the boy and his parents *had* come aboard last night. It wasn't going to be quite the peaceful trip he had hopefully visualised – not with that toddler around. But Dr McPhee smiled at the memory of the boy in motion. Another little extra to freighter life and an added interest to counter those endless days of steaming that lay ahead. Yes. He had put off an holiday for far too long –

'Dr McPhee! Over here! Please ...'

Electricity and sunlight made the room over bright but he instantly placed the loud clear voice even before he saw Mrs Halliwell. He moved through the clutter of tables to the only one that sat four – the Captain's table. And *he* had just departed judging by the evidence: a lingering smell of cigar smoke, the silver coffee-pot and a half filled cup. Mrs Halliwell followed Dr McPhee's glance and said casually, 'What a pity you missed Captain Prins. Such a nice man and he speaks perfect English. He had to do something on the bridge, I think. This is the third time we've had breakfast at his table, isn't it, Clare?'

Dr McPhee noted once again what a steady blue gaze Clare Halliwell had. She was a plump pink-cheeked fifteen year old, and a striking contrast to her angular, faded mother who must have been well into her forties. Clare was going home to finish her education in England ... 'Bishop's High School may be the best school in Georgetown. But it is still only a *colonial* education.' That was the way her mother had put it yesterday. The girl had said very little in his presence, so far – but then her mother gave her hardly a chance. Yet he had instantly liked the quiet young girl.

Now, Clare said, 'Yes, Mummy. Three times ...' Then she

lowered the steady blue eyes and cut into a sausage on her plate.

'Would you recommend the sausages, Clare?' Dr McPhee smiled at the girl and she went a brighter shade of pink before she said softly, 'They are very good ...'

So he ordered sausages and tomatoes, toast and coffee, from the steward who was suddenly at his elbow. He had just relaxed with a contented sigh when the early morning toddler came pattering into his thoughts – 'Oh, by the way, I now have a few neighbours – in cabin three.' Dr McPhee looked at Mrs Halliwell. 'Picked them up last night, I hear. I was asleep before ten. It has to be this bracing sea-air that doctors are always recommending. Must be something in it, after all!'

Clare smiled but her mother sat forward eagerly. 'Well, you missed our one and only port of call. And Paramaribo was very interesting, wasn't it, Clare? The wharf – oh, Captain Prins said the Dutch word is *stelling* – was full of lights and people. Very bright and merry, almost like a carnival. And it was after one o'clock in the morning! Now there's nothing more to see until Southampton. We've got another eighteen days of sailing ahead. Or is it *nineteen*, Clare?'

'Eighteen,' the girl said quietly.

Mrs Halliwell nodded, stirred her coffee, and watched Dr McPhee being served. The steward was deftly efficient; the breakfast cleanly served and piping hot. Dr McPhee set to with a will. Then the four sugar planters jostled their way into the dining saloon and sat themselves down glumly at a couple of tables. They had all obviously had another night of solid drinking. The rumour was that they had brought aboard two cases of Demerara rum and were determined to empty the last bottle before docking at Southampton. Dr McPhee, cutting into a delicious sausage, wondered wryly if it were at all possible to keep anything secret on a freighter like the *Hollander*. He decided it just wasn't possible and watched the young steward march smartly over to the morose four. Then he brought his attention back to the two women and smiled at them both. 'So the final passenger count is ten, I take it? Including one little boy who gets up at daybreak and runs around!'

'Oh, you've seen him!' There was a sharp edge of

disapproval to Mrs Halliwell's loud voice. "The boy's *black*, Dr McPhee. The longer I live in the West Indies, the more I'm sure that mixed marriages are very wrong. They shouldn't be. I'm sorry, Dr McPhee ... but I believe in plain speaking and that is my decided opinion!'

'One should always have an opinion,' Dr McPhee agreed mildly, forking half a sausage, 'but whether one should offer it aloud is debatable, to say the least.' Mrs Halliwell was obviously going to be rather a trying fellow passenger. But it was a long sail ahead and so polite detachment was the necessary treatment. Thirty years of medical practice had given a smooth polish to such a stance. He wouldn't allow the woman to penetrate that. Dr McPhee swallowed and again brought Clare into the conversation – 'The sausages *are* delicious. Dutch ones, I think. Would you pour me a cup of coffee, my dear?'

Again Clare coloured fiercely and she kept her eyes down as she poured. 'Fine. No milk, no sugar ...' Clare placed the cup and saucer beside his plate.

'Thank you.'

And then unexpectedly, Clare said. 'The passenger list is now *nine*. The boy hasn't a mother, it was his father who brought him aboard last night. He carried the boy ... he was asleep. I wonder if his father will bring him in to breakfast?' It was the first time that Clare had spoken at length.

Dr McPhee sipped the strong black coffee then slowly lowered his cup back on the saucer.

'Are you quite sure? Wasn't there a woman? Tall, very slim – and black?'

'Well, they went right past us,' Mrs Halliwell said. She moulded her thin lips into a pale disapproving line. 'And I'm quite relieved that there isn't such a person on board. Quite relieved, Dr McPhee!'

'I see. Well, I naturally assumed that a toddler would travel with his mother – and father.' He smiled blandly at the two women while clear logic told him that he couldn't possibly have seen a tall, slim, black girl, with her back against the door to the after-deck. Not if she hadn't come aboard last night. And then his eyes met Clare's steady blue gaze and Dr McPhee knew instantly that she, too, had seen *something*.

By mid-morning, he knew what Clare had seen.

She was suddenly by his side as he stood leaning over the rail and gazing, wilfully mesmerised, into the blue-green water. Dr McPhee turned with a start, then settled his glasses with a forefinger and smiled encouragingly at the girl. 'I think you have something to tell me. What is it, Clare?'

But he was still unprepared for what the girl actually said: 'There *was* someone – a woman, as you said. She followed the man and the little boy. She was right behind them as they came aboard. It took me a little while before I realised that no one else was seeing her. Just *me* ...' Clare stopped and brought her blue eyes up from the sea, tilting up her round pink face. 'Did she frighten you, Dr McPhee?'

'No, I didn't feel anything of the sort. Rather sad, perhaps, but that's about all. *I* saw her this morning in the passage to the cabins. She seemed to be just keeping an eye on the boy. You do realise that we're standing here calmly talking about a – a ghost?' But Clare's gaze remained steady and she nodded. 'Yes, I know. But I feel exactly as you do – about her. Oh! Here comes mummy and she looks as if she needs help ...' And Clare moved quickly over to her mother.

Mrs Halliwell was burdened with a blanket, two books and a parasol – and news that she was longing to broadcast. Even before she was fully settled in one of the two deck-chairs, her voice was being borne down-wind ...

'Dr McPhee, your neighbour in cabin three is an Englishman! Naturally, as he came aboard at Paramaribo, I took him to be Dutch. He didn't speak a word last night, did he, Clare? Well, he's English and his name is Jonathan Carey. He's some sort of agricultural chemist and he was in Surinam on a three year contract – keeping the pests away from the Dutch sugar-canes.' By now she was fully settled but suddenly Mrs Halliwell sat upright – 'Clare! My cushion! I left it in the cabin ... and you know just how my back plays up without it. Do fetch it for me, will you?'

'Yes, mummy,' Clare said, and left obediently.

'She's a good girl,' Mrs Halliwell said smugly. 'But her puppy fat worries me so. She will lose it, won't she, Dr McPhee? The women on my side of the family are all slim. I can't stand great fat women.'

'You've no cause to worry. She'll be fine. She's unusually mature for her age, Mrs Halliwell.'

Clare's mother took the last comment as a personal compliment. 'Yes, she is, isn't she? But this is just the age to get her back to England and true civilisation. Mr Halliwell and I both agree that Clare must stay on with my sister in Norfolk and finish her schooling there. It's a wrench, naturally ... but who can she marry in a West Indian city like Georgetown? Oh! That reminds me – *your* Mr Carey got himself mixed up with a local girl and the result is that little boy he brought aboard last night. He should be ashamed of himself – '

'And the child's mother is dead, I take it?'

'Oh yes.' Mrs Halliwell's lips made the thin pale line again and she flicked open the parasol like a swordsman making a thrust. 'The wages of sin – as the good book says. Did you know that our young cabin steward speaks very good English? His name is Jan Vandel. Such a nice boy. Loves a good chat to better his English. Oh! I do wish that Clare would hurry up. I can't sit comfortably in a deckchair without a cushion ...'

'I'll see what I can do,' Dr McPhee said and before she could protest he had opened the door on the afterdeck and stepped smartly into the passage between the cabins. There was a sudden roar like a cannon broadside from cabin six where the sugar planters were crowded. Packed like drunken sardines, Dr McPhee thought, and smiled at the idea. Clare and her mother occupied a cabin at the far end and, stooping slightly, he started in that direction. But the tall black girl was there, ahead of him, still and listening, standing in a sunlit pool cast by a porthole ...

She was before the door of cabin three and from inside the cabin Dr McPhee could now hear a soothing voice. Clare's. 'Come on now,' the girl was saying, 'Do take your bottle. *Yes.* Like that. Good boy ... you're a good little boy, aren't you?'

And Dr McPhee still moving resolutely on, found himself at the door of cabin three – and *alone.* He had no idea at what precise moment the tall black girl had vanished. But vanished she had. The ship's engines thumped steadily on, the heaving sea was out there, just beyond the thin hull ... and right here, Dr McPhee thought, something is happening for which there is no explanation. Not a medical one, anyway.

Clare looked around as he came into the cabin.

'I heard the little boy making a choking sound ... it was his bottle. But he's fine now, drinking away like mad. Look at him! Oh, gosh! Is mummy looking for me? Her cushion ...'

He smiled down at the crouching girl, holding the bottle to the boy's mouth as he lay flat on the lower bunk, a high rail keeping him firmly in. He was sucking vigorously while one chubby hand stroked Clare's face. Now his round dark eyes swung up and over to look at Dr McPhee – and then they went beyond Dr McPhee.

The boy worked his lips free of the teat and smiled wide and suddenly. Then he cried, '*De moeder!*'

Simultaneously, Clare and Dr McPhee looked around. There was no one else in the cabin. The boy contentedly took the teat back into his mouth and again patted Clare on the cheek. At that moment someone did join them in the cabin for Jan, the young cabin steward, said, 'He drinks, eh? I did not stay for his father say he feeds himself, yes?' Jan came further in and looked down at the boy and Clare. 'Miss ... I stay now until his father is back from the shower.'

Clare coloured vividly as always but she seemed determined to know just one thing. 'What does *De moeder* mean?' she asked. Dr McPhee waited, too, but thought he knew the answer.

'In English? – mother!'

The girl nodded, satisfied. Then – 'Oh, gosh! That reminds me – the cushion!' And in a moment she had stood up and edged her way to the cabin door. 'I'll see you later, Dr McPhee. 'Bye, little boy!' Then she was gone.

'Well, I must go too, Jan. Mr Carey won't like a stranger here when he returns from the shower.' He looked at the bright open face of the Dutch youth. 'Does the little chap call out to his mother very often? By name?'

'Yes and yes,' Jan said, suddenly looking thoughtful. 'Many times. As if she is here. His father say he will forget to remember very soon!'

Dr McPhee nodded and adjusted his slipping glasses. 'Quite true. It's just a matter of time. I think I'll have a little nap before lunch. I'm glad you're keeping an eye on the boy.

Quite a handful.' He nodded cheerfully at Jan and stepped out of the cabin and went into his own and shut the door. Then he moved over to the open porthole and sniffed the heady mixture of salt and sea and hot oil. The sun poured in like an oversized penny ... and it was impossible to think that the slim ghost of a dead woman was still sharing it all.

Yet Dr McPhee knew now that she *was*.

And at dinner that night he met Jonathan Carey for the first time. The toddler's father was already at the table allotted to Dr McPhee – and the Chief Engineer. (Captain Prins had scattered his crew members, very democratically, among the dining tables of the passengers, but the crew were proving very erratic eaters.) Tonight there was no Chief Engineer. Dr McPhee nodded at Captain Prins and Mrs Halliwell, then gave Clare a warm conspiratorial smile. The girl coloured but her blue eyes never wavered. He wondered with amusement whether the Captain *had* chosen Mrs Halliwell (and Clare) as permanent guests at his table. He doubted if the Captain had had much choice in the matter. But Dr McPhee was certain about one thing – nothing would budge Clare's mother from her privileged position until they docked at Southampton.

Dr McPhee introduced himself and Jonathan Carey shook hands. He was a slim young man with a mass of tousled blond hair and the look of a distracted scoutmaster who had just counted heads to find himself a cub short. It was the kind of look any father would acquire, Dr McPhee reasoned, battling with a toddler on his own. They chatted through the meal – to be exact, Dr McPhee tried to keep a conversation going, but it was only at the sweet course that his companion suddenly seized on a fact –

'Sorry – but you did say you were a doctor? I'm glad we've got one on board. It's my son. I do worry about him falling ill. You know how it is ...' Jonathan Carey's voice trailed off and his glance grew vague again.

'Your son looks perfectly healthy to me. I've seen him twice today. Please don't worry on that score. Much more to the point ... you should see that he doesn't go overboard!' And Dr McPhee was pleased when the boy's father smiled. 'Jan – our cabin steward – has already done something about that. He's made a kind of harness ... a bit of rope and a wide leather belt.

I'll put it to the test tomorrow when I take him out on deck!'
Animated, he was an extremely pleasant young man. The
boyish, rather helpless kind, that women seem to cherish. And
one woman *had*. Also, their off-spring, even after death –

Precisely at that moment, Jonathan Carey said, 'Theo's
mother died quite suddenly, you see. Two months ago. I still
find it hard to believe that she *is* dead. Now, I keep worrying
about Theo – and what do I do with him?' They had reached
the sweet course and now he abruptly pushed aside the
untouched bowl of fruit-salad and stood up. 'I'm sorry. I feel I
must go. Theo's asleep – but you know how children are ...
Goodnight, Doctor!'

'Yes, of course. Good night, Mr Carey!'

A few minutes later Clare had made her way to his table
and was standing at Dr McPhee's elbow. 'Please, may I join
you? Mummy isn't having any coffee, she says it keeps her
awake and she hears the noise from number six – the sugar
planters' cabin. So may I have mine with you?' Clare waved
back to her mother but Mrs Halliwell's eyes were fixed on the
bland red face of Captain Prins as he talked. Dr McPhee
smiled at Clare. 'Of course, my dear. Do sit down. The
steward will be back in a minute ...'

Clare took the seat Jonathan Carey had so recently vacated,
then she said with quiet drama, 'Did you know that his wife
died of a heart attack? He woke one morning to find her dead
beside him ... and the little boy was crying in the next room. It
must have been awful for him. She was a Dutch subject and
when he arrived in Surinam to take up that agricultural post,
they met and fell in love ...' Clare faltered then and her round
face grew slowly scarlet. 'Well, I – I'm sure that they *did*.
Aren't you?'

'Quite sure,' Dr McPhee said, smiling. 'By the way, the
boy's name is Theo ...' And at Clare's look of surprise, he
laughed. 'At least I *can* make a contribution to the general
gossip. And where did you hear all this?'

Clare moved her plump shoulders.

'Mummy ... where else? And *she* had it all from Jan, our
cabin steward. He's yours, too, isn't he? He and mummy are
great friends already. It's odd how most of the crew speak
English. And all I know in Dutch is *De moeder*! I think it's the

only word that you know, too ...' And Clare smiled her grave
slow smile.

Dr McPhee nodded and as the steward had returned to the
table, he ordered coffee. 'Theo!' Clare said. 'What a curious
name. I'll bet that it was *her* choice ...'

And from the next day, Theo took over the crew, the ship –
and Clare Halliwell.

Dr McPhee watched it happen with quiet enjoyment. The
little chocolate coloured toddler became the nearest thing to a
ship's mascot. A privileged mascot who went everywhere ...
always watched over and endlessly indulged. On the afterdeck he laughed in the wind and sunshine, held securely on
the end of his harness. For, once in motion, Theo was very
much like that runaway train going downhill – even to the
hooting. The wide leather strap across his sturdy chest and
the long rope attached to it, saved him a dozen times a day
from going headlong over the side. The rope was sometimes
anchored, very short, on the wall fixture that carried a lifebelt;
more often, Clare stood laughing and holding firmly to the
rope while Theo played.

Theo also had the run of the cabins. In the dining-saloon
the First Engineer (with Jan Vandel's help) had rigged up an
impromptu high-chair, by elevating a small canvas one on
four lengths of wood. In it, Theo held court at mealtimes,
joining in the laughter when he fed his mashed potatoes into
his right ear. Or chubby hands taking a glass of milk as the
room cheered him on. Then Theo joining in the clapping,
after he had drained his glass without spilling more than a
quarter of the milk.

'Theo! It's always Theo!'

Mrs Halliwell made a grimace of distaste and moved her
head back under the shade of the parasol. 'That child has
ruined the voyage for me. He really has. And do you know, Dr
McPhee, that Clare was the quietest little girl? Never a sound
from her at *his* age. Oh, I forgot ... *you* like little Theo, don't
you?'

Dr McPhee lay in the other deck-chair, in full sunlight,
letting the loud voice wash serenely over him. The past ten
days of ship-board intimacy had confirmed his worst fears

about Mrs Halliwell. She was the type of Englishwoman who should have stayed safely at home with her dislikes and prejudices. That she had emerged safely from eight years of Colonial life, spoke volumes about the placidity of the native population.

'Oh, come now ... you are enjoying yourself, surely?'

He smiled at Clare's mother and thought fondly of Clare. How could one female beget another so unlike herself? Medically, at least, Dr McPhee knew of no answer. He tried a new conversational track – 'I brought a few back copies of *The Manchester Guardian* aboard with me – I receive the paper regularly in Georgetown – and it does say that the decorations in the Abbey will stay up for quite a few months after the Coronation. And those along the Mall, too. So Clare can visualise it all for herself – '

Very loudly, Mrs Halliwell cut him short – 'Not quite the same thing! We wanted to be in London for June 2nd and watch our young Queen being crowned ... but all passages from Georgetown were fully booked well into 1954. We were lucky to get aboard the *Hollander* this year. Thank God for freighters that take passengers!' And she wasn't to be side-tracked for long – 'You do realise, of course, with everyone on board playing Nanny to his little black boy, the father is free to take up drinking – or haven't you noticed that, Dr McPhee?'

Dr McPhee had. The four sugar planters had indeed recruited Jonathan Carey for their drinking sessions, but he decided that one loud condemning voice was enough. Instead he squinted under his wind-blown white hair and said mildly, 'The poor chap has had a rough time of it. He certainly isn't the kind to cope alone with a small boy – not one like Theo. And as for Theo, just think what the last ten days would have been like if that little rascal hadn't come aboard?'

'I *can*,' Mrs Halliwell snapped with deep feeling, 'and the word is *peaceful*!' And when Dr McPhee threw back his head and laughed heartily, she collected her book and cushion, got up with a great show of dignity, and went through the door to the cabins.

That evening Dr McPhee was on deck, quietly smoking his after dinner pipe. He liked the calm of the ship at this particular hour ... the gurgle and swish of the sea, the salted wind slapping his face and the sound of the ship's engine, steady as a healthy heart-beat.

And then Clare was at his elbow. This had grown into a nightly habit and she actually *liked* the smell of pipe-tobacco, as she had told him in her grave way. 'Hello, Dr McPhee!'

'Theo is sound asleep, I take it?'

Clare nodded, smiling faintly as she looked down into the night dark sea. 'Did you know that *her* name was – Saskia? Such a lovely name to say ...' Clare turned on the rail and looked at Dr McPhee with her level blue gaze. 'Have you seen her since that first time?' She was wearing a white dress that showed up the freckled pink of her firm round arms. 'I saw her again – just once – the morning that Theo – '

'Choked on his bottle? I did, too!'

'She was at the door of the cabin, then I heard the choking sounds – and the next moment she was gone! Do you know what I think? I think that she's happy now because Theo is happy! There isn't any need now to – to *materialise*. Is that the right word?'

'Yes.' He smiled at Clare. He liked her best when the grave grown-up role slipped and the enthusiastic child peeped through. 'Well, the trip is more than halfway over ... everything's set fair, I think.' He puffed meditatively then he said, 'I've got my own fancies about her, too. For one thing, I call her ... the silent stowaway! Silent and watchful and quite powerless. I'm quite sure of the last ...'

He saw Clare nod her head in agreement.

'I think I would have liked her if we'd met when she ...' The wind blew the rest of Clare's words away, or perhaps she had just stopped. They stayed in companionable silence for a little while then the girl said, 'Mummy said ten minutes. Goodnight, Dr McPhee!'

'Good night, Clare!'

He watched her go and thought for the hundredth time: why hadn't I provided a daughter for my old age? A thought that had never occurred to him until boarding the *Hollander* and meeting Clare Halliwell. Dr McPhee sighed for what might have been – knocked his pipe out on the rail and left the afterdeck to spray, wind and stars. As he prepared to contort himself to fit the narrow bunk he heard the muffled noise from cabin six – the sugar planters, plus their new drinking recruit, Jonathan Carey. Dr McPhee, clicking off the bunk-light, thought briefly of Mrs Halliwell, listening and seething impotently, and smiled in the darkness. Then he fell asleep. The new, deep, uninterrupted sleep that his profession had made an occasional luxury, until now ...

The next morning, Clare was tapping on his door the moment he got back from the shower. 'A beautiful day! Oh, You're still in your dressing-gown ...' She stood at the cabin door, glowing with excitement. 'Do you know the day and the date?'

'Let's see ... Monday the 25th! Month – August! Right or wrong? It's difficult to keep track on an Ancient Mariners' voyage, like this one!'

'Correct about the date!' Then Clare bubbled over with her news – 'And it's Theo's birthday! He's two today – his father just said so. And there's to be a birthday party at tea-time. A cake, candles, and everything. Jan Vandel is arranging it all with the Chef ... isn't it marvellous?'

'Yes, it is,' Dr McPhee said, smiling at the girl's excitement and catching a bit of it too. 'Is everyone invited? Am I?'

'Everyone – from two to a hundred!' Clare's blue eyes were alight. 'Theo will go mad with joy! Now, don't forget, will you? I know that you never bother with afternoon tea. But today you *must* ... the dining saloon at four!'

After Clare had gone he closed the cabin door and stood thinking for a moment, hands tugging at the cord of the dressing-gown. Did Clare realise that she hadn't specified – *only the living*? Would Saskia come to her son's birthday party? Dr McPhee doubted that she could stay away ...

And she didn't.

At tea-time the dining saloon was crammed to its polished walls: all passengers (including the sugar planters), most of the crew (including the Chef, not seen in the very solid flesh until now), and the guest of honour and his father. Theo was in high spirits, thoroughly enjoying, as always, being the centre of any event. And this event was truly his. He clapped his hands, smiled, and made a valiant attempt at blowing out the two fat red candles on the huge iced cake. Clare showed

him how to blow ... his father showed him, too – but the
flames only flickered when the little boy puffed his cheeks and
blew, in imitation of the grown-ups –

'Come on, Theo!'

'Blow, boy! *Blow!*'

'That's it, Theo! You can do it!'

But again the flames only bent then slowly came back to the
straight bright lines. Theo was delighted with his failures. He
clapped his hands and laughed then looking straight ahead he
gave a shout of delight –

'*De moeder!*' Theo said, as clear as a bell.

And Dr McPhee, standing behind Clare and Jonathan
Carey, could see the tall black girl, smiling over the heads of
those crowding close on the opposite side of the table. She was
smiling at Theo, her dark eyes, lustrous and loving. And as Dr
McPhee watched, the tall black girl arched her slender neck
forward and silently blew out the candles ...

Someone else in the shouting, jostling crowd that
surrounded the table, may have done it. But Dr McPhee was
certain *she* had ... he had seen the smile slowly disappear as
Saskia shaped her lips for the blow ... then the candle flames
bent, twisted and went out, trailing long wisps of thin grey
smoke. And when Dr McPhee looked up from the cake the tall
black girl was slowly disappearing, exactly like the smoke
from the candles. Then she had faded completely – leaving
only the flushed faces of the sugar planters and, behind them,
the smiling one of the Chief Engineer.

It was a great birthday party.

Everyone agreed that it must have been one of the best at
sea. But it was against Mrs Halliwell's nature not to speak her
mind – 'Those fat red candles looked quite *wrong*. Left over
from Christmas, I'm sure. Couldn't they find proper birthday
ones?'

'Oh, Mummy! Please!' Clare tried hard not to sound
exasperated. 'Poor Jan Vandel had an awful time finding any
at all. But those pastries, and jelly, and ice-cream ...' Clare
sighed in weary joy and then her steady gaze was on Dr
McPhee's face. 'For a time I thought that Theo would never
be able to blow out his candles. Didn't you feel the same?'

Her clear gaze was very steady.

'No. I could see that someone would help him ...' And when Clare smiled her grave smile, Dr McPhee was sure. '*You* wanted everyone there – and everyone came!'

'Well, I think that boy ate far too much of everything,' Mrs Halliwell commented and sniffed at the memory. 'But his kind is never taught not to be greedy. The boy will be sick, you mark my words!'

'Very likely,' Dr McPhee said, and realised that for the very first time he had actually agreed with Clare's mother. 'Anyway, *I* shan't be coming in to dinner. My stomach needs a long rest. I have some lecture notes to write up so I'll just stay in my cabin and then make an early night of it.'

And that is what he did. But he awoke suddenly in the faint light of the cabin, knowing that a presence was there. Saskia's presence – and that *she* had willed him awake. And now he could see her, a slim tall shadow against the cabin door. Then beyond the wall he heard Theo crying: soft whimpers of pain and distress. He reached for the light cord, found it and pulled. With the bright light the shadow had vanished from the door.

Dr McPhee paused only to put on his glasses and search his bag, then he went next door with a bottle of Magnesia.

Theo was asleep in half an hour. Dr McPhee's liking for children markedly increased when they were unwell. He was soothing and gentle and firm – and the Magnesia helped. Finally, he peered down at the relaxed little boy with wry amusement; really, the boy was the most adaptable creature he'd ever come across. It was clear that Theo would settle quite happily with a wandering pigmy tribe, deep in the Amazonas. So what of a new life in England?

Dr McPhee chuckled and went back to his cabin, then he got into his dressing-gown and went down the passage to cabin six. At his single sharp rap, the door was opened the merest crack, but cigarette smoke and a low masculine rumble of voices leaked out – and the pungent smell of rum.

'Ah, my friend the doctor!' Jock Sinclair blearily recognised him at last. 'Would you join us for a wee drink?' He opened the door wider but Dr McPhee shook his head. 'Thank you – but no. I have a message for Mr Carey, if he's here. His son needs him. I think he should go to his cabin immediately – and stay there! Good night – or rather, *Good morning!*' Then Dr McPhee turned on his slippered heels and went marching back to his cabin. It didn't take him long to go back to sleep but, before he did, he heard the soft clicks as the door of the next cabin opened and closed.

In the morning, Theo was his usual clock-work driven self, pattering away up and down the passage, giving a fat chuckle at every tumble. Then came a light indecisive knock on Dr McPhee's cabin door.

'Come in ...'

But it wasn't the young Jan Vandel with the morning tea. Jonathan Carey stood in the doorway, unshaved, fully dressed, and decidedly sheepish. Dr McPhee guessed correctly that he had lain on his top bunk exactly as he was. He obviously hadn't done any sleeping either. 'Good morning, Doctor. I – I just wanted to say, thank you – ' But by then Theo had pattered his way in, swaying like a drunken sailor, hands, as usual, high over his curly black head. His father watched as Theo made a few dizzy circles, then he said vaguely, 'Everyone's been so kind. But he's my responsibility, I do know that. And I *have* been letting things slide a bit, lately. I'm truly sorry about last night ...'

Dr McPhee had got himself smoothly out of his bunk (twelve days and nights of practice had perfected the act), and reached for his glasses. Now he looked thoughtfully down at Theo. 'Quite a handful, isn't he? What do you plan to do when you get to England? Who's going to take care of him?'

There was a lengthy pause while Jonathan Carey wearily opened and closed his eyes. 'My mother, I hope. She knew of my marriage in Surinam but she never approved. I wrote to her when Saskia died that I'd decided to come home but I didn't tell her that I had Theo with me –'

'Is that wise? Surely the last thing you should do is to spring the boy on your mother like that? Particularly if she hadn't – approved – of your marriage to a local girl!'

Jonathan Carey stroked his wild blond hair and groaned.

'God! I can't think! I've got a bit of a headache. Please excuse me and – and thank you again for last night.' Then he abruptly herded Theo out of the cabin and back into his. Dr

McPhee shut his own cabin door and thoughtfully prepared to go for his morning shower.

Theo's father was certainly a problem, one way or the other.

And he remained a problem during the next six days as the *Hollander* drew ever nearer to Southampton. Dr McPhee checked daily (and discreetly) with Mr Breitner, the wireless operator, but always – 'No ... Mynheer Carey did not wire a message to England.'

Finally, he told Clare what he had found out the morning after Theo's birthday party – 'Oh! You never said that he'd been sick ...' Clare could only think of the toddler. 'You should have rapped on our door ... you knew that I'd come!' Then she paused and asked quietly, 'Dr McPhee – how did you know that Theo was ill?'

'*She* woke me, of course ... Saskia!'

Together they listened to the wash of the sea and the thump of the engines. At last, Clare said, 'And you do think that Mr Carey should wire his mother, so that she will know that Theo's coming, too? Is that it?'

Dr McPhee pulled on his bed-time pipe. 'Don't you? It's better to know just how she feels about her grandson *now* – than later, when he arrives on her doorstep.'

Clare took a deep swallow of the night wind. 'I promise that I'll make him send that wire. He'll do it tomorrow morning while I'm dressing Theo. Please don't worry any more.' She was so quietly matter-of-fact that Dr McPhee felt the wire was as good as sent. 'Dr McPhee, how often have you seen Saskia since the night Theo was ill?'

He peered at the girl and Clare was looking back at him, intently and steadily. 'Every day since then. At Theo's door. Here, on deck ... just tonight, at dinner, right behind the boy's high chair!'

'I do, too. Nearly every day ...' Clare sighed into the night. 'She must be very unhappy again. Poor, poor Saskia!' She turned, leant against the rail, and looked up at Dr McPhee. 'It's very strange that it's just us two who can see her. Not mummy ... not any of the other passengers. None of the crew – not even Theo's father! Well, good night! I'll let you know the latest at breakfast ...'

And Clare went quietly and in a few minutes Dr McPhee knocked his pipe out and followed.

Next morning Clare came into the dining saloon leading Theo by the hand. She was aglow with her triumph. 'Mr Carey is with the wireless operator. He'll join you in a few minutes.' She lifted Theo with ease into the high chair. 'Must join mummy *instantly*... she still gets furious that I dress Theo. The steward will bring his porridge in a moment.' Clare patted the curly head – 'Now you be good! *And* eat your porridge without making a mess ...'

The boy kicked his legs high then banged her on the arm with his spoon.

'You'd better go, my dear – before he makes you a casualty!' Dr McPhee took the flying hand and said with mock severity, 'That's enough, young man! You'll wait to be served *quietly* like everyone else ...'

And when, a few minutes later, Jonathan Carey joined them, Dr McPhee knew that the cable had gone off at last. The young man was alert and smiling broadly. 'Good morning, doctor!' He kissed his son on the forehead and was rewarded by a whack from the spoon. He sat down laughing. 'By the way, do you know that tonight's dinner is rather special ... the Captain's farewell and all that? It's at a later time, so I'll put my son to bed before it all starts. Our young friend, Jan, will give Theo his supper in the cabin. I don't know how I would have got through this trip without that Dutch boy – and Clare Halliwell, of course!' He had even managed to get his hair under control for it lay flat and wet and shining. 'And here's the steward with the porridge. Thank you – now, Theo ... slowly, *please.*' Then Jonathan Carey turned briskly round. 'And what are you having for breakfast, doctor? Let's settle for scrambled eggs with sausages *and* tomatoes. I've never felt so hungry.'

Indecision, Dr McPhee thought, can be as debilitating as a disease. But much more easily cured. He smiled and said, 'Why not? I'm hungry, too.'

And that was the moment Theo threw a spoonful of porridge on his father's shirt. Jonathan Carey mopped up the mess, laughing heartily.

Mrs Halliwell was full of plans for the two days in London before travelling on to Norfolk. 'Fancy! Southampton is less than forty-eight hours away. When we sailed from British Guiana I just couldn't believe that there'd *be* an end to this voyage. Now, it's almost over – bar the Captain's dinner tonight!' She peered around from under the parasol. 'Have you seen Clare, Dr McPhee?'

Lunch was over and they were in the deck-chairs; now he closed his book and squinted into the sunlight. 'She took Theo back for his afternoon nap.' Today, for some reason, Mrs Halliwell *was* penetrating his armour of non-committal politeness. When she sniffed loudly and rattled the parasol, Dr McPhee knew he had to escape. 'And that reminds me that I should have one too. This *is* a convalescence trip – and I have to keep reminding myself that it is!' He heaved himself to his feet and adjusted his slipping glasses, then he marched for the door into the passage.

The loud shrill voice caught up with him – 'You won't forget the farewell dinner, will you?'

'I'll be there,' Dr McPhee called back and seriously thought of missing the thing and having a light supper tray in his cabin. But the idea was instantly dismissed as too impolite – and from the very start, the Captain and crew members of the *Hollander* set out to make the evening one that the passengers would long remember. Small twin flags, of the Netherlands and Great Britain, decorated each table ... and each table was honoured by a crew member. Dr McPhee and Jonathan Carey had the Chief Engineer, at last: beefy, red-faced, gold-rimmed glasses, and near perfect English. Even before the first course he had started to tell Dr McPhee, with total recall, details of the abdominal operation he had had the previous year ...

At the Captain's table, Mrs Halliwell was like a brilliant humming-bird in rainbow coloured silk. Clare looked extra plump and subdued in a long, close-fitting red dress, that would have been ideal for a woman over thirty. Poor girl. Her mother's choice, no doubt, Dr McPhee thought sympathetically. Then the dinner started with a bang and *schnapps*.

The menu managed to be both stodgy and superb; Dutch cooking at its best and the meal went on for a very long time indeed. The four sugar planters, sharing tables with the Chief Purser *and* the Second Mate, all grew progressively merrier. Voices, laughter, and the thickening fog of cigars and cigarettes. And finally, after refusing his sixth Dutch cigar, Dr McPhee decided he needed the support of his pipe. He left the dining saloon and climbed, very carefully, to the deck and fresh air, and made his way to the passengers' cabins. He had drunk quite a lot and felt happy, expansive, and at peace with his floating world. And so was quite unprepared to see her so plainly. In such *living* detail.

The two passage lights were on and Saskia stood, head tilted on her slender neck, as if listening for a sound from the cabin in which Theo slept. The tall slim body in the blue cotton dress, the features, gauntly European ... and the dark, large, lustrous eyes. Eyes that were suddenly gazing directly at Dr McPhee ...

At that moment, the ship's generators missed a beat, the lights flickered, as they had done a hundred times before, and then Saskia wasn't there. He may have involuntarily blinked, with the sharp flicker of the lights ... but she had vanished in the space of that flicker.

Dr McPhee got his pipe, opened the door of cabin three and crossed to the lower bunk where Theo was soundly sleeping, in a wild disorder of sheets, blanket and pillow. Quietly he left and as quietly rejoined the bedlam of the dining saloon. But not for long. He was already back in his cabin when the dinner finally came to an end and the passengers and crew dispersed with much hand-shaking, back-slapping, and chaste kisses on the cheeks of the two females.

By then, too, Dr McPhee had already worded the message he intended sending by wireless to his sister in Herne Hill, London, alerting her of his imminent arrival. But the morning would do. Dr McPhee put his glasses safely away, clicked out the bunk-light and was almost instantly asleep.

And for the first time since coming aboard the *Hollander*, he overslept.

It was after ten o'clock in the morning when Dr McPhee awoke. He couldn't believe his heavy eyes when he squinted at his wrist-watch. The morning tea in the blue and white china that Jan Vandel had quietly placed on the ledge by the bunk-head, was cold to his experimental sip. He grimaced and put the cup down. Shaving and a shower would have to wait; he *had* to send that wire off to London. He dressed with the old professional speed, but feeling out of joint with the morning – the bright, sea-salt taste of it ... feeling oddly like the last man left aboard.

Once outside his cabin, Dr McPhee lost the feeling. Mrs Halliwell's voice filtered clearly through from the afterdeck. Jan Vandel was whistling softly as he tidied up a cabin two doors away. There was the solid thud of Theo's feet racing across the deck, and Clare's happy laugh. Get the best out of today, Dr McPhee thought, it's your last day at sea. He suddenly felt amazingly nostalgic for this mode of living that would vanish forever by night and landfall. Then he made his way forward to the Bridge and the wireless room.

Captain Prins met him at the top, smiling broadly. 'You are well, doctor?' It was a heavy joke that the Captain always tried out whenever they met.

'Not very. I shall have to see a doctor!' And Dr McPhee again gave the accepted answer and was rewarded by a fat chuckle.

Then he turned on the bridge and headed for the door of the wireless room. The door opened as he got there and Mr Breitner stepped out into the sunshine. 'Ah! Just the man I want. May I send a wire to London?

'But, yes. Of course. You have the message and the address?' Mr Breitner held out a large white hand and took the sheet. 'And now, dokter ... you will please to give *this* message to Mynheer Carey?'

'Delighted to be of service, my dear Mr Breitner!' Dr McPhee took the small sheet that the wireless operator was now holding out. 'I'll see that he gets it right away. Oh, there's no answer to my wire. Good-bye – and thank you ...' And Dr McPhee turned and climbed carefully back to the flat firmness of the deck. Once there, he glanced quickly at the neatly blocked-in words that made up the message. It stood out shockingly clear from the printed section of the sheet and Dr McPhee read:

> *SS Hollander*
> DATE: September 1st 1953
> TIME: 10.00 Hrs
> MESSAGE: The Child Is Not Wanted
> SENDER: Rosalind Carey (Mevrouw)

At that moment the unease he had felt on awakening crystallized into a sudden irrational panic. Dr McPhee read the note again, this time in a slow motion of dread ... and he knew that he was not reading it alone. Saskia was at his elbow, peering over both shoulders. Everywhere ...

She knew.

Dr McPhee spun wildly to right, then left; did a full circle, but she wasn't to be seen. For the first time, Saskia was a force only to be *felt.* And he instantly knew something else, that he had been horribly wrong about her; his stomach muscles dissolved into icy matter with the knowledge. Gentle, brooding and forlorn she may have appeared – but impotent, that Saskia had never been!

And it was too late.

From the afterdeck Mrs Halliwell's voice came loudly but edged with a shrill urgency: 'Clare! You've dropped the rope! Look at the child ...'

Even at such a moment he was amazed at the concern in the voice, and when Dr McPhee looked across the expanse of deck and battened-down hatches, he too shouted at Clare –

'The lead! Clare! *Pick it up!*'

But his strange voice, almost too weak to carry on the wind, didn't move the girl either. Clare was standing rigid in the sunlight, the wind whipping her hair in a frenzied mass across her blank face, while her hands stayed limply at her side. And again Mrs Halliwell's voice, now almost a scream of terror –

'Theo! Oh, God! Catch the boy, someone ...'

For Theo, the rope from his harness trailing snake-like across the deck, was in full unstoppable motion, heading straight for the forbidden rails and the sheer drop beyond.

Dr McPhee shouted again. But only the weak croaking ...

'Clare! *Clare ...*'

He watched in a kind of frozen disbelief as Jonathan Carey suddenly shot forward, grabbing frantically at his running son. And something tripped Jonathan Carey for he suddenly crashed his full length on the deck, with Theo just a few inches from his clutching hands. At that moment the boy seemed to leap upwards – or was snatched upwards – and stayed high over the rails for a few agonizing seconds, then Theo had gone clearly over the side of the *Hollander*. And his father, scrambling to his feet, was wailing in a high childish shout: 'My son's overboard! My son's overboard ...'

Dr McPhee found that he could move and think normally again, while panicky, noisy activity began to rage around him. A banshee hooting from the funnels, a mad clanging of bells, then the jolt and shiver of engines cutting out on command, and running feet and barked orders. And all the time he was struggling to get to Clare's side. There was a full crowd now, thick and silent at the rails, when he finally reached the afterdeck. But Clare stood alone, on the fringe of the crowd, exactly as Dr McPhee had seen her when her mother's voice had first made him look up and over.

'Clare! *Clare!*'

When he took her by the rounded shoulders, he could see that the blue eyes were fixed and glazed with shock. He shook her, hard. Then he freed a hand a slapped her across the cheeks. Twice. Her head jerked with each slap but when she swung back to face him, her eyes were coming alive – and the memory was beginning to dilate them. Then she fell against his chest, weeping like a small child. He gave her a minute of grief –

'Clare ... you must come with me back to your cabin. I'll give you something to make – '

Clare looked up, her eyes still wide with horror. 'Saskia – *she* tugged the rope away ... you know that, don't you? I couldn't see her and this time she – was *frightening*!' The girl fought a sob, swallowed, then she said in slow disbelief, 'Dr McPhee, she – she threw Theo overboard! She couldn't have loved him, after all! Not the way *we* did. *Why?* How could a mother do such a thing?'

Clare started to cry again.

He knew that this was not the moment for answers. Later he would show her the wireless message in his shirt pocket. But not now. 'Clare! Come, my dear ...'

She came with him, still sobbing, and before they went through the door in the afterdeck, Dr McPhee looked back at the silent crowd at the rails, watching a life-boat being jerkily lowered to a grey choppy sea. His last glimpse was of a surprising duo: Mrs Halliwell and Jonathan Carey stood a little apart from the crowd and Clare's mother had a thin arm across the heaving, hunched shoulders of Theo's father.

The *Hollander* docked at Southampton, eight hours late – with one passenger listed as missing: *Theo Philip Carey, aged two*. The log carried no entry of a stowaway found on the voyage – alive or dead. The two people who could have spoken of Saskia, parted forever at Southampton, without mentioning her name. Or Theo's.

There has been silence ever since ...

VII

The Realm of the Unreal
Ambrose Gwinnett Bierce

Ambrose Gwinnett Bierce (1838-1914?) was a mystery writer of
great merit. Again his tales show the sure touch of the craftsman
combined with a fertile and original imagination. Perhaps his
greatest mystery was his eventual death for during the Mexican
revolution in 1914 he took himself off there to join Pancho Villar's
forces, and was never again heard of!

For a part of the distance between Auburn and Newcastle the
road – first on one side of a creek and then on the other –
occupies the whole bottom of the ravine, being partly cut out
of the steep hillside, and partly built up with boulders
removed from the creek-bed by the miners. The hills are
wooded, the course of the ravine is sinuous. In a dark night
careful driving is required in order not to go off into the water.
The night that I have in memory was dark, the creek a torrent,
swollen by a recent storm. I had driven up from Newcastle
and was within about a mile of Auburn in the darkest and
narrowest part of the ravine, looking intently ahead of my
horse for the roadway. Suddenly I saw a man almost under
the animal's nose, and reined in with a jerk that came near
setting the creature upon its haunches.

'I beg your pardon,' I said, 'I did not see you, sir.'

'You could hardly be expected to see me,' the man replied
civilly, approaching the side of the vehicle; 'and the noise of
the creek prevented my hearing you.'

I at once recognised the voice, although five years had
passed since I had heard it. I was not particularly well pleased
to hear it now.

'You are Dr Dorrimore, I think,' said I.

'Yes; and you are my good friend Mr Manrich. I am more
than glad to see you – the excess,' he added, with a light

laugh, 'being due to the fact that I am going your way, and naturally expect an invitation to ride with you.'

'Which I extend with all my heart.'

That was not altogether true.

Dr Dorrimore thanked me as he seated himself beside me, and I drove cautiously forward, as before. Doubtless it is fancy, but it seems to me now that the remaining distance was made in a chill fog; that I was uncomfortably cold; that the way was longer than ever before, and the town, when we reached it, cheerless, forbidding, and desolate. It must have been early in the evening, yet I do not recollect a light in any of the houses nor a living thing in the streets. Dorrimore explained at some length how he happened to be there, and where he had been during the years that had elapsed since I had seen him. I recall the fact of the narrative, but none of the facts narrated. He had been in foreign countries and had returned – this is all that my memory retains, and this I already knew. As to myself I cannot remember that I spoke a word, though doubtless I did.

Of one thing I am distinctly conscious: the man's presence at my side was strangely distasteful and disquieting – so much so that when I at last pulled up under the lights of the Putnam House I experienced a sense of having escaped some spiritual peril of a nature peculiarly forbidding. This sense of relief was somewhat modified by the discovery that Dr Dorrimore was living at the same hotel.

In partial explanation of my feelings regarding Dr Dorrimore I will relate briefly the circumstances under which I had met him some years before. One evening a half-dozen men of whom I was one were sitting in the library of the Bohemian Club in San Francisco. The conversation had turned to the subject of sleight-of-hand and the feats of the *prestidigitateurs*, one of whom was then exhibiting at a local theatre.

'These fellows are pretenders in a double sense,' said one of the party. 'They can do nothing which it is worth one's while to be made a dupe by. The humblest wayside juggler in India could mystify them to the verge of lunacy.'

'For example, how?' asked another, lighting a cigar.

'For example, by all their common and familiar

performances – throwing large objects into the air which never come down; causing plants to sprout, grow visible and blossom, in bare ground chosen by spectators; putting a man into a wicker basket, piercing him through and through with a sword while he shrieks and bleeds, and then – the basket being opened, nothing is there; tossing the free end of a silken ladder into the air, mounting it and disappearing.'

'Nonsense!' I said, rather uncivilly, I fear. 'You surely do not believe such things?'

'Certainly not; I have seen them too often.'

'But I do,' said a journalist of considerable local fame as a picturesque reporter. 'I have so frequently related them that nothing but observation could shake my conviction. Why, gentlemen, I have my own word for it.'

Nobody laughed – all were looking at something behind me. Turning in my seat I saw a man in evening dress who had just entered the room. He was exceedingly dark, almost swarthy, with a thin face, black-bearded to the lips, an abundance of coarse black hair in some disorder, a high nose and eyes that glittered with as soulless an expression as those of a cobra. One of the group rose and introduced him as Dr Dorrimore, of Calcutta. As each of us was presented in turn he acknowledged the fact with a profound bow in the Oriental manner, but with nothing of Oriental gravity. His smile impressed me as cynical and a trifle contemptuous. His whole demeanour I can describe only as disagreeably engaging.

His presence led the conversation into other channels. He said little – I do not recall anything of what he did say. I thought his voice singularly rich and melodious, but it affected me in the same way as his eyes and smile. In a few minutes I rose to go. He also rose and put on his overcoat.

'Mr Manrich,' he said, 'I am going your way.'

'The devil you are!' I thought. 'How do you know which way I am going?' Then I said, 'I shall be pleased to have your company.'

We left the building together. No cabs were in sight, the street cars had gone to bed, there was a full moon and the cool night air was delightful; we walked up the California Street Hill. I took that direction thinking he would naturally wish to take another, towards one of the hotels.

'You do not believe what is told of the Hindu jugglers,' he said abruptly.

'How do you know that?' I asked.

Without replying he laid his hand lightly upon my arm and with the other pointed to the stone sidewalk directly in front. There, almost at our feet, lay the dead body of a man, the face upturned and white in the moonlight! A sword whose hilt sparkled with gems stood fixed and upright in the breast; a pool of blood had collected on the stones of the sidewalk.

I was startled and terrified – not only by what I saw, but by the circumstances under which I saw it. Repeatedly during our ascent of the hill my eyes, I thought, had traversed the whole reach of that sidewalk, from street to street. How could they have been insensible to this dreadful object now so conspicuous in the white moonlight?

As my dazed faculties cleared I observed that the body was in evening dress; the overcoat thrown wide open revealed the dress-coat, the white tie, the broad expanse of shirt front pierced by the sword. And – horrible revelation! – the face, except for its pallor, was that of my companion! It was to the minutest detail of dress and feature Dr Dorrimore himself. Bewildered and horrified, I turned to look for the living man. He was nowhere visible, and with an added terror I retired from the place, down the hill in the direction whence I had come. I had taken but a few strides when a strong grasp upon my shoulder arrested me. I came near crying out with terror: the dead man, the sword still fixed in his breast, stood beside me! Pulling out the sword with his disengaged hand, he flung it from him, the moonlight glinting upon the jewels of its hilt and the unsullied steel of its blade. It fell with a clang upon the sidewalk ahead and – vanished! The man, swarthy as before, relaxed his grasp upon my shoulder and looked at me with the same cynical regard that I had observed on first meeting him. The dead have not that look – it partly restored me, and turning my head backward, I saw the smooth white expanse of sidewalk, unbroken from street to street.

'What is all this nonsense, you devil?' I demanded, fiercely enough, though weak and trembling in every limb.

'It is what some are pleased to call jugglery,' he answered, with a light, hard laugh.

He turned down Dupont Street and I saw him no more until we met in the Auburn ravine.

On the day after my second meeting with Dr Dorrimore I did not see him: the clerk in the Putnam House explained that a slight illness confined him to his rooms. That afternoon at the railway station I was surprised and made happy by the unexpected arrival of Miss Margaret Corray and her mother, from Oakland.

This is not a love story. I am no storyteller, and love as it is cannot be portrayed in a literature dominated and enthralled by the debasing tyranny which 'sentences letters' in the name of the Young Girl. Under the Young Girl's blighting reign – or rather under the rule of those false Ministers of the Censure who have appointed themselves to the custody of her welfare – Love

veils her sacred fires,
And, unaware, Morality expires,

famished upon the sifted meal and distilled water of a prudish purveyance.

Let it suffice that Miss Corray and I were engaged in marriage. She and her mother went to the hotel at which I lived, and for two weeks I saw her daily. That I was happy needs hardly be said; the only bar to my perfect enjoyment of those golden days was the presence of Dr Dorrimore, whom I had felt compelled to introduce to the ladies.

By them he was evidently held in favour. What could I say? I knew absolutely nothing to his discredit. His manners were those of a cultivated and considerate gentleman; and to women a man's manner is the man. On one or two occasions when I saw Miss Corray walking with him I was furious, and once had the indiscretion to protest. Asked for reasons, I had none to give, and fancied I saw in her expression a shade of contempt for the vagaries of a jealous mind. In time I grew morose and consciously disagreeable, and resolved in my madness to return to San Francisco the next day. Of this, however, I said nothing.

There was at Auburn an old, abandoned cemetery. It was nearly in the heart of the town, yet by night it was as gruesome a place as the most dismal of human moods could crave. The railings about the plots were prostrate, decayed, or altogether gone. Many of the graves were sunken, from others grew sturdy pines, whose roots had committed unspeakable sins. The headstones were fallen and broken across; brambles overran the ground; the fence was mostly gone, and cows and pigs wandered there at will: the place was a dishonour to the living, a calumny on the dead, a blasphemy against God.

The evening of the day on which I had taken my madman's resolution to depart in anger from all that was dear to me found me in that congenial spot. The light of the half moon fell ghostly through the foliage of trees in spots and patches, revealing much that was unsightly, and the black shadows seemed conspiracies withholding to the proper time revelations of darker import. Passing along what had been a gravel path, I saw emerging from shadow the figure of Dr Dorrimore. I was myself in shadow, and stood still with clenched hands and set teeth, trying to control the impulse to leap upon and strangle him. A moment later a second figure joined him and clung to his arm. It was Margaret Corray!

I cannot rightly relate what occurred. I know that I sprang forward, bent upon murder; I know that I was found in the grey of the morning, bruised and bloody, with finger marks upon my throat. I was taken to the Putnam House, where for days I lay in a delirium. All this I know, for I have been told. And of my own knowledge I know that when consciousness returned with convalescence I sent for the clerk of the hotel.

'Are Mrs Corray and her daughter still here?' I asked.

'What name did you say?'

'Corray.'

'Nobody of that name has been here.'

'I beg you will not trifle with me,' I said petulantly. 'You see that I am all right now; tell me the truth.'

'I give you my word,' he replied with evident sincerity, 'we have had no guests of that name.'

His words stupefied me. I lay for a few moments in silence; then I asked: 'Where is Dr Dorrimore?'

'He left on the morning of your fight and has not been heard of since. It was a rough deal he gave you.'

Such are the facts of this case. Margaret Corray is now my wife. She has never seen Auburn, and during the weeks whose history as it shaped itself in my brain I have endeavoured to relate, was living at her home in Oakland, wondering where her lover was and why he did not write. The other day I saw in the *Baltimore Sun* the following paragraph:

Professor Valentine Dorrimore, the hypnotist, had a large audience last night. The lecturer, who has lived most of his life in India, gave some marvellous exhibitions of his power, hypnotising anyone who chose to submit himself to the experiment, by merely looking at him. In fact, he twice hypnotised the entire audience (reporters alone exempted), making all entertain the most extraordinary illusions. The most valuable feature of the lecture was the disclosure of the methods of the Hindu jugglers in their famous performances, familiar in the mouths of travellers. The professor declares that these thaumaturgists have acquired such skill in the art which he learned at their feet that they perform their miracles by simply throwing the 'spectators' into a state of hypnosis and telling them what to see and hear. His assertion that a peculiarly susceptible subject may be kept in the realm of the unreal for weeks, months, and even years, dominated by whatever delusions and hallucinations the operator may from time to time suggest, is a trifle disquieting.

VIII

The Buick Saloon
Ann Bridge

*Ann Bridge's tale is set in the China of the early 1930s, in a Peking
very different of course from the Communist capital of today. It was a
time when the European domination of Chinese business life was
widespread, and the cosmopolitan atmosphere of the period, in a land
where life was cheap and tinted with a certain mystery, add to the
fascination this tale has for me today.*

To Mrs James St George Bernard Bowlby it seemed almost
providential that she should recover from the series of illnesses
which had perforce kept her in England, at the precise
moment when Bowlby was promoted from being No 2 to
being No 1 in the Grand Oriental Bank in Peking. Her
improved health and his improved circumstances made it
obvious that now at last she should join him, and she wrote to
suggest it. Bowlby of course agreed, and out she came. He
went down to meet her in Shanghai, but business having
called him further still, to Hong Kong, Mrs Bowlby proceeded
to Peking alone, and took up her quarters in the big ugly grey-
brick house behind the Bank in Legation Street. She tried, as
many managers' wives had tried before her, to do her best
with the solid mahogany and green leather furniture provided
by the Bank, wondering the while how Bowlby, so dependent
always on the feminine touch on his life and surroundings,
had endured the lesser solidities of the sub-manager's house
alone for so long. She bought silks and black-wood and scroll-
paintings. She also bought a car. 'You'll need a car, and you'd
better have a saloon, because of the dust,' Bowlby had said.

People who come to Peking without motors of their own seldom buy new ones. There are always second-hand cars going, from many sources: the leavings of transferred diplomatists, the jetsam of financial ventures, the sediment of conferences. So one morning Mrs Bowlby went down with Thompson, the new No 2 in the Bank, to Maxon's garage in the Nan Shih Tzu to choose her car. After much conversation with the Canadian manager they pitched on a Buick saloon. It was a Buick of the type which is practically standard in the Far East, and had been entirely repainted outside, a respectable dark blue; the inside had been newly done up in a pleasant soft grey which appealed to Mrs Bowlby. The manager was loud in its praises. The suspension was excellent ('You want that on these roads, Mrs Bowlby') – the driver and his colleague sat outside ('Much better, Mr Thompson. If these fellows have been eating garlic – they shouldn't, but they do – '). Thompson knew they did, and agreed heartily. Mrs Bowlby, new to such transactions, wanted to know who the car had belonged to. The manager was firmly vague. This was not a commission sale – he had bought the car when the owners left. Very good people – 'from the Quarter.' This fully satisfied Thompson, who knew that only Europeans live (above the rose, anyhow) in the Legation Quarter of Peking.

So the Buick saloon was bought. Thompson, having heard at the club that the late Grand Oriental chauffeur drank petrol, did not re-engage him with the rest of the servants according to custom, but secured instead for Mrs Bowlby the chauffeur of a departing manager of the Banque Franco-Belge. By the time Bowlby returned from Hong Kong the chauffeur and his colleague had been fitted out with khaki livery for winter, with white for summer – in either case with trim gold cuff- and hat-bands – and Mrs Bowlby, in her blue saloon, had settled down to pay her calls.

In Peking the newcomer calls first; a curious and discouraging system. It is an ordeal even to the hardened. Mrs Bowlby was not hardened; she was a small, shy, frail woman, who wore grey by preference, and looked grey – eyes, hair, and skin. She had no idea of asserting herself; if she had things in her – subtleties, delicacies – she did not wear them outside;

she did not impose herself. She hated the calls. But as she was also extremely conscientious, day after day, trying to fortify herself by the sight of the two khaki-and-gold figures in front of her, exhaling their possible garlic to the outer air beyond the glass partition, she called. She called on the diplomats' wives in the Quarter; she called on 'the Salt' (officials of the Salt Gabelle); she called on the Customs – English, Italian, American, and French; she called on the Posts – French, Italian, American, and English. The annual displacement of pasteboard in Peking must amount to many tons, and in this useful work Mrs Bowlby, alone in the grey interior of her car, faithfully took her share. She carried with her a little list on which, with the help of her Number One boy (as much a permanent fixture in the Bank house, almost, as the doors and windows), she had written out the styles, titles, and addresses of the ladies she wished to visit. The late chauffeur of the Banque Franco-Belge spoke excellent French; so did Mrs Bowlby – it was one of her few accomplishments; but as no Chinese can or will master European names, the European needs must learn and use the peculiar versions current among them. 'Ta Ch'in chai T'ai-t'ai, Turkuofu,' read out Mrs Bowlby when she wished to call on the wife of the German Minister. '*Oui, Madame!*' said Shwang. 'Pei T'ai-t'ai, Kung Hsien Hutung,' read out Mrs Bowlby when visiting Mrs Bray, the Doctor's wife; but when she wished to call on Mrs Bennett, the wife of the Commandant of the English Guard, and Mrs Baines, the Chaplain's wife, she found that they were both *Pei T'ai-t'ai* too – which led to confusion.

It began towards the end of the first week. Possibly it was her absorption in the lists and the Chinese names that prevented her from noticing it sooner, but at the end of that week Mrs Bowlby would have sworn that she heard French spoken beside her as she drove about. Once, a little later, as she was driving down the Rue Marco Polo to fetch her husband from the Club, a voice said '*C'est lui!*' in an underbreath, eagerly – or so she thought. The windows were lowered, and Mrs Bowlby put it down to the servants in front. But it persisted. More than once she thought she heard a soft sigh. 'Nerves!' thought Mrs Bowlby – her nerves were always a menace to her, and Peking, she knew, was bad for them.

She went on saying 'Nerves' for two or three more days; then, one afternoon, she changed her mind. She was driving along the Ta Chiang an Chieh, the great thoroughfare running east and west outside the Legation Quarter, where the trams ring and clang past the scarlet walls and golden roofs of the Forbidden City, and long lines of camels, coming in with coal from the country as they have come for centuries, cross the road between the Dodges and Daimlers of the new China.

It was a soft brilliant afternoon in April, and the cinder track along the glacis of the Quarter was thronged with riders; polo had begun, and as the car neared Hatamen Street she caught a glimpse of the white-and-scarlet figures through the drifting dust on her right. At the corner of the Hatamen the car stopped; a string of camels was passing up to the great gate-way, and she had to wait. She sat back in the car, glad of the pause; she was unusually moved by the loveliness of the day, by the beauty and strangeness of the scene, by the whole magic of spring in Peking. She was going later to watch the polo, a terrifying game; she wished Jim didn't play.

Suddenly, across her idle thoughts, a voice beside her spoke clearly. '*Au revoir*!' it said, '*mon très-cher! Ne tombe pas, je t'en prie.*' And as the car moved forward behind the last of the camels, soft and unmistakable there came a sigh, and the words, '*Ce polo! Quel sport affreux! Dieu, que je le déteste!*' in a passionate undertone.

'That *wasn't* the chauffeur!' was what Mrs Bowlby found herself saying. The front windows were up. And that low, rather husky voice, the cultivated and clear accent, could not be confounded for a moment with Shwang's guttural French. Besides, what chauffeur would talk like that? The thing was ridiculous. 'And it *wasn't* nerves, this time,' said Mrs Bowlby, her thoughts running this way and that round the phenomenon. 'She did say it. Then it was she who said "*C'est lui*!" before,' she said almost triumphantly, a moment later.

Curiously, though she was puzzled and startled, she realised presently that she was not in the least frightened. That someone with a beautiful voice should speak French in her car was absurd and impossible, but it wasn't alarming. In her timid way Mrs Bowlby rather prided herself on her common sense, and as she shopped and called she considered this extraordinary occurrence from all the common-sense points of view that she could think of, but it remained a baffling and obstinate fact. Before her drive was over she found herself wishing simply to hear the voice again. It was ridiculous, but she did. And she had her wish. As the car turned into Legation Street an hour later she saw that it was too late to go to the polo; the last chukka was over, and the players were leaving the ground, over which dust still hung in the low brilliant light, in cars and rickshas. As she passed the gate the voice spoke again – almost in front of her, this time, as though the speaker were leaning forward to the window. '*Le voilà!*' it said – and then, quite loudly '*Jacques!*' Mrs Bowlby almost leaned out of the window herself, to look for whoever was being summoned – as she sat back, conscious of her folly, she heard again beside her, quite low, '*Il ne m'a pas vue.*'

There was no mistake about it. It was broad daylight; there she was in her car, bowling along Legation Street – past the Belgian Bank, past the German Legation; rickshas skimming in front of her, Mme de Réan bowing to her. And just as clear and certain as all these things had been this woman's voice, calling to Jacques, whoever he was – terrified lest he should fall at polo, hating the game for his sake. What a lovely voice it was! Who was she, Mrs Bowlby wondered, and what and who was Jacques? '*Mon très-cher!*' she had called him – a delicious expression. It belonged to the day and the place – it was near to her own mood as she had sat at the corner of the Hatamen and noticed the spring, and hated the polo too for Jim's sake. She would have liked to call Jim '*mon très-cher,*' only he would have been so surprised.

The thought of Bowlby brought her up with a round turn. What would he say to this affair? Instantly, though she prolonged the discussion with herself for form's sake, she knew that she was not going to tell him. Not yet, anyhow. Bowlby had not been very satisfied with her choice of a car as it was – he said it was too big and too expensive to run. Besides, there was the question of her nerves. If he failed to hear the voice too she would be in a terribly difficult position. But there was more to it than that. She had a faint sense that she had been eavesdropping, however involuntarily. She had no right to give away even a voice which said '*mon très-cher*' in that tone.

This feeling grew upon her in the days that followed. The voice that haunted the Buick became of almost daily occurrence, furnishing a curious secret background to her social routine of calls and 'At Homes.' It spoke always in French, always to or about Jacques – a person, whoever he was, greatly loved. Sometimes it was clear to Mrs Bowlby that she was hearing only half of a conversation between the two, as one does at the telephone. The man's voice she never heard, but, as at the telephone, she could often guess at what he said. Much of the speech was trivial enough: arrangements for meetings at lunches, at the polo; for week-end parties at Pao-ma-chang in the temple of this person or that.

This was more eerie than anything else to Mrs Bowlby – the hearing of plans concerned with people she knew. '*Alors, dimanche prochain, chez les Milne.*' Meeting '*les Milne*' soon after, she would stare at them uneasily, as though by looking long enough she might find about them some trace of the presence which was more familiar to her than their own. Her voice was making ghosts of the living. But whether plans, or snatches of talk about people or ponies, there came always, sooner or later, the undernote of tenderness, now hesitant, now frank – the close concern, the monopolising happiness of a woman in love.

It puzzled Mrs Bowlby that the car should only register, as it were, the woman's voice. But then the whole affair bristled with puzzles. Why did Bowlby hear nothing? For he did not – she would have realised her worst fears if she *had* told him. She remembered always the first time that the voice spoke when he was with her. They were going to a *thé dansant* at the Peking Hotel, a farewell party for some Minister. As the car swung out of the Jade Canal Road, past the policemen who stand with fixed bayonets at the edge of the glacis, the voice began suddenly, as it so often did, in French – 'Then I leave thee now – thou wilt send back the car?' And as they lurched across the tramlines towards the huge European building and pulled up, it went on, 'But tonight, one will dance, *n'est ce pas?*'

'Goodness, what a crowd!' said Bowlby. 'This is going to be

simply awful. Don't let's stay long. Will half an hour be enough, do you think?'

Mrs Bowlby stared at him without answering. Was it possible? She nearly gave herself away in the shock of her astonishment. 'What's the matter?' said Bowlby, 'What are you looking at?'

Bowlby had not heard a word!

She noticed other things. There were certain places where the voice 'came through', so to speak, more clearly and regularly than elsewhere. Intermittent fragments, sometimes unintelligible, occurred anywhere. But she came to know where to expect to hear most. Near the polo ground, for instance, which she hardly ever passed without hearing some expression of anxiety or pride. She often went to the polo, for Jim was a keen and brilliant player; but it was a horror to her while he played, and this feeling was a sort of link, it seemed to her, between her and her unseen companion. More and more, too, she heard it near the Hatamen and in the *hu-t'ungs* or alleys to the east of it.

Mrs Bowlby liked the East City. It lies rather in a backwater, between the crowded noisy thoroughfare of Hatamen Street, with its trams, dust, cars, and camels, and the silent angle of the Tartar Wall, rising above the low one-storey houses. A good many Europeans live there, and she was always glad when a call took her that way, through the narrow *hu-t'ungs* where the car lurched over heaps of rubbish or skidded in the deep dust, and rickshas pulled aside into gateways to let her pass. Many of these lanes end vaguely in big open spaces, where pigs root among the refuse and little boys wander about, singing long monotonous songs with a curious jerky rhythm in their high nasal voices. Sometimes, as she waited before a scarlet door, a flute-player out of sight would begin to play, and the thin sweet melody filled the sunny air between the blank grey walls. Flowering trees showed here and there above them; copper-smiths plied their trade on the steps of carved marble gate-ways; dogs and beggars sunned themselves under the white and scarlet walls of temple courtyards. Here, more than anywhere else, the voice spoke clearly, freely, continuously, the rapid rounded

French syllables falling on the air from nowhere, now high, light, and merry, with teasing words and inflection, now sinking into low murmurs of rapturous happiness. At such times Mrs Bowlby sat wholly absorbed in listening, drawn by the lovely voice into a life not her own and held fascinated by the spell of this passionate adventure. Happy as she was with Bowlby, her life with him had never known anything like this. He had never wanted, and she had never dared to use the endearments lavished by the late owner of the Buick saloon on her Jacques.

She heard enough to follow the course of the affair pretty closely. They met where they could in public, but somewhere in the Chinese City there was clearly a meeting-place of their own – '*Notre petit asile*'. And gradually this haven began to take shape in Mrs Bowlby's mind. Joyous references were made to various features of it. Tomorrow they would drink tea on the stone table under 'our great white pine'. There was the fish-pond shaped like a shamrock, where one of the goldfish died – '*pourtant en Irelande celà porte bonheur, le trèfle, n'est ce pas?*' The parapet of this pond broke away and had to be repaired, and Jacques made some sort of inscription in the damp mortar, for the voice thrilled softly one day as it murmured – '*Maintenant il se lit là pour toujours, ton amour!*' And all through that enchanted spring, first the lilac bushes perfumed the hours spent beneath the pine, and then the acacias that stood in a square round the shamrock pond. Still more that life and hers seemed to Mrs Bowlby strangely mingled; her own lilacs bloomed and scented the courtyard behind the grey Bank building, and one day, as they drove to lunch in the British Legation, she drew Jim's attention to the scent of the acacias, which drowned the whole compound in perfume. But Bowlby said, with a sort of shiver, that he hated the smell; and he swore at the chauffeur in French, which he spoke even better than his wife.

The desire grew on Mrs Bowlby to know more of her pair, who and what they were and how their story ended. But it seemed wholly impossible to find out. Her reticence made her quite unequal to setting anyone on to question the people at the garage again. And then one day, accidentally, the clue was given her. She had been calling at one of the houses in the

French Legation; the two house servants, in blue-and-silver gowns, stood respectfully on the steps; her footman held open the door of the car for her. As she seated herself the voice said in a clear tone of command, '230, Por Hua Shan Hut'ung!' Acting on an impulse which surprised her, Mrs Bowlby repeated the order – '*Deux cent trente, Por Hua Shan Hut'ung,*' she said. Shwang's colleague bowed and shut the door. But she caught sight, as she spoke, of the faces of the two servants on the steps. Was it imagination? Surely not. She would have sworn that a flicker of some emotion – surprise, and recollection – had appeared for a moment on their sealed and impassive countenances. In Peking the servants in Legation houses are commonly handed on from employer to employer, like the furniture; and the fact struck on her with sudden conviction – they had heard those words before!

Her heart rose with excitement as the car swung out of the compound into Legation Street. Where was it going? She had no idea where the Por Hua Shan Hut'ung was. Was she about to get a stage nearer to the solution of the mystery at last? At the Hatamen the Buick turned south along the glacis. So far so good. They left the Hatamen, bumped into the Suchow Hut'ung, followed on down the Tung Tsung Pu Hut'ung, right into the heart of the East City. Her breath came fast. It must be right. Now they were skirting the edge of one of the rubbish-strewn open spaces, and the East Wall rose close ahead of them. They turned left, parallel with it; turned right again towards it; stopped. Shwang beckoned to a pancake-seller who was rolling out his wares in a doorway, and a colloquy in Chinese ensued. They went on, slowly, then, down a lane between high walls which ended at the Wall's very foot, and pulled up some hundred yards off it before a high scarlet door, whose rows of golden knobs in fives betokened the former dwelling of some Chinese of rank.

It was only when Liu came to open the door and held out his cotton-gloved hand for her cards that Mrs Bowlby realised that she had no idea what she was going to do. She could not call on a voice! She summoned Shwang; Liu's French was not his strong point. 'Ask,' she said to Shwang, 'who lives here – the T'ai-t'ai's name.' Shwang rang the bell. There was a long pause. Shwang rang again. There came a sound of shuffling feet inside; creaking on its hinges the door opened, and the head of an old Chinaman, thinly bearded and topped with a little black cap, appeared in the crack. A conversation followed, and then Shwang returned to the car.

'The house is empty,' he said.

'Ask him who lived there last,' said Mrs Bowlby.

Another and longer conversation followed, but at last Shwang came to the window with the information that a foreign *T'ai-t'ai*, '*Fa-kuo T'ai-t'ai*' (French lady), he thought, had lived there, but she had gone away. With that Mrs Bowlby had to be content. It was something. It might be much. The car had moved on towards the Wall, seeking a place to turn, when an idea struck her. Telling Shwang to wait, she got out, and glanced along the foot of the Wall in both directions. Yes! Some two hundred yards from where she stood one of those huge ramps, used in former times to ride or drive up onto the summit of the Wall, descended into the dusty strip of waste land at its foot. She hurried towards it, nervously, picking her way between the rough fallen lumps of stone and heaps of rubbish; she was afraid that the servants would regard her action as strange, and that when she reached the foot of the ramp she might not be able to get up it. Since Boxer times the top of the Tartar Wall is forbidden as a promenade, save for a short strip just above the Legation Quarter, and the ramps are stoutly closed at the foot, theoretically. But in China theory and practice do not always correspond, Mrs Bowlby knew; and as she hurried, she hoped.

Her hope was justified. Though a solid wooden barrier closed the foot of the ramp, a few feet higher up a little bolt-hole, large enough to admit a goat or a small man, had been picked away in the masonry of the parapet. Mrs Bowlby scrambled through and found herself on the cobbled slope of the ramp; panting a little, she walked up it on to the Wall. The great flagged top, broad enough for two motor-lorries to drive abreast, stretched away to left and right; a thick undergrowth of thorny bushes had sprung up between the flagstones, and through them wound a little path, manifestly used by goats and goat-herds. Below her Peking lay spread out – a city turned by the trees which grow in every courtyard into the semblance of a green wood, out of which rose the immense golden roofs of the Forbidden City; beyond it, far away, the faint mauve line of the Western Hills hung on the sky. But Mrs Bowlby had no eyes for the unparalleled view.

Peeping cautiously through the battlements she located the Buick saloon, shining incongruously neat and modern in its squalid and deserted surroundings; by it she took her bearings, and moved with a beating heart along the little path between the thorns. Hoopoes flew out in front of her, calling their sweet note, and perched again, raising and lowering their crests; she never heeded them, nor her torn silk stockings. Now she was above the car: yes, there was the lane up which they had come, and the wall beyond it was the wall of that house! She could see the door-keeper, doll-like below her, still standing in his scarlet door-way, watching the car curiously. The garden wall stretched up close to the foot of the City Wall itself so that, as she came abreast of it, the whole compound – the house, with its manifold courtyards, and the formal garden – lay spread out at her feet with the minute perfection of a child's toy farm on the floor.

Mrs Bowlby stood looking down at it. A dream-like sense of unreality came over her, greater than any yet caused even by her impossible voice. A magnificent white pine, trunk and branches gleaming as if white-washed among its dark needles, rose out of the garden, and below it stood a round stone table among groups of lilacs. Just as the voice had described it! Close by, separated from the pine garden by a wall pierced with a fan-shaped door-way was another, with a goldfish pond shaped like a shamrock, and round it stood a square pleached alley of acacias. Flowers in great tubs bloomed everywhere. Here was the very setting of her lovers' secret idyll; silent, sunny, sweet, it lay under the brooding protection of the Tartar Wall. Here she was indeed near to the heart of her mystery, Mrs Bowlby felt, as she leaned on the stone parapet, looking down at the deserted garden. A strange fancy came to her that she would have liked to bring Jim here and people it once again. But she and Jim, she reflected with a little sigh, were staid married people, with no need of a secret haven hidden away in the East City. And with the thought of Jim the claims of everyday life reasserted themselves. She must go – and with a last glance at the garden she hastened back to the car.

During the next day or so Mrs Bowlby brooded over her new discovery and all that had led to it. Everything – the place where the address had been given by the voice, the flicker of recognition on the faces of the servants at the house in the French Legation, the fact of the door-keeper in the East City having mentioned a *Fa-kuo t'ai-t'ai* as his late employer, pointed to one thing – that the former owner of the Buick saloon had lived in the house where she had first called on that momentous afternoon. More than ever, now, the thing took hold of her – having penetrated the secret of the voice so far, she felt that she must follow it further yet. Timid or not, she must brace herself to ask some questions.

At a dinner a few nights later she found herself seated next to Mr van Adam. Mr van Adam was an elderly American, the *doyen* of Peking society, who had seen everything and known everyone since before Boxer days – a walking memory and a mine of social information. Mrs Bowlby determined to apply to him. She displayed unwonted craft. She spoke of Legation compounds in general, and of the French compound in particular; she praised the garden of the house where she had called. And then:

'Who lived there before the Vernets came?' she asked, and waited eagerly for the answer.

Mr van Adam eyed her a little curiously, she thought, but replied that it was a certain Count d'Ardennes.

'Was he married?' Mrs Bowlby next enquired.

Oh yes, he was married right enough – but the usual reminiscent flow of anecdote seemed to fail Mr van Adam in this case. Struggling against a vague sense of difficulty, of a hitch somewhere, Mrs Bowlby pushed on nevertheless to an enquiry as to what the Comtesse d'Ardennes was like.

'A siren!' Mr van Adam replied briefly – adding, 'Lovely creature, though, as ever stepped.'

He edged away rather from the subject, or so it seemed to Mrs Bowlby, but she nerved herself to another question – 'Had they a car?'

Mr van Adam fairly stared, at that; then he broke into a

laugh. 'Car? Why yes – she went everywhere in a yellow Buick – we used to call it "the canary".'

The talk drifted off onto cars in general, and Mrs Bowlby let it drift; she was revolving in her mind the form of her last question. Her curiosity must look odd, she reflected nervously; it was all more difficult, somehow, than she had expected. Her craft was failing her – she could not think of a good excuse for further questions that would not run the risk of betraying her secret. There must have been a scandal – there *would* have been, of course; but Mrs Bowlby was not of the order of women who in Peking ask coolly at the dinner-table, 'And what was *her* scandal?'

At dessert, in desperation, she put it hurriedly, baldly, 'When did the d'Ardennes leave?'

Mr van Adam paused before he answered, 'Oh, going on for a year ago, now. She was ill, they said – looked it, anyway – and went back to France. He was transferred to Bangkok soon after, but I don't know if she's gone out to him again. The East didn't suit her.'

'Oh, poor thing!' murmured Mrs Bowlby, softly and sincerely, her heart full of pity for the woman with the lovely voice and the lovely name, whose failing health had severed her from her Jacques. Not even love such as hers could control this wretched feeble body, reflected Mrs Bowlby, whom few places suited. The ladies rose, and too absorbed in her reflections to pay any further attention to Mr van Adam, she rose and went with them.

At this stage Mrs Bowlby went to Pei-t'ai-ho for the summer. Peking, with a temperature of over 100 degrees in the shade, is no place for delicate women in July and August. Cars are not allowed on the sandy roads of the pleasant straggling seaside resort, and missionaries and diplomatists alike are obliged to fall back on rickshas and donkeys as means of locomotion. So the Buick saloon was left in Peking with Jim, who came down for long week-ends as often as he could.

Thus separated from her car, and in changed surroundings, Mrs Bowlby endeavoured to take stock of the whole affair dispassionately. Get away from it she could not. Bathing, idling on the hot sunny beach, walking through the green paths bordered with maize and kaoliang, sitting out in the blessedly cool dark after dinner, she found herself as much absorbed as ever in this personality whose secret life she so strangely shared. Curiously enough, she felt no wish to ask any more questions of anyone. With her knowledge of Mme d'Ardennes' name the sense of eavesdropping had returned in full force. One thing struck her as a little odd: that if there *had* been a scandal she should not have heard of it – in Peking, where scandals were innumerable, and treated with startling openness and frank disregard. Perhaps she had been mistaken, though, in Mr van Adam's attitude, and there had not been one. Or – the illumination came to her belated and suddenly – hadn't Mr van Adam's son in the Customs, who went home last year, been called Jack? He had! And Mrs Bowlby shuddered at the thought of her clumsiness. She could not have chosen a worse person for her enquiries.

Another thing, at Pei-t'ai-ho, she realised with a certain astonishment – that she had not been perceptibly shocked by this intrigue. Mrs Bowlby had always believed herself to hold thoroughly conventional British views on marriage; the late owner of the Buick saloon clearly had not, yet Mrs Bowlby had never thought of censuring her. She had even been a little resentful of Mr van Adam's calling her a siren. Sirens were cold-hearted creatures, who lured men frivolously to their doom; her voice was not the voice of a siren. Mrs Bowlby was all on the side of her voice. Didn't such love justify itself, argued Mrs Bowlby, awake at last to her own moral failure to condemn another, or very nearly? Perhaps, she caught herself thinking, if people knew as much about all love affairs as she knew about this one, they would be less censorious.

Mrs Bowlby stayed late at Pei-t'ai-ho, well on into September, till the breezes blew chilly off the sea, the green paths had faded to a dusty yellow, and the maize and kaoliang were being cut. When she returned to Peking she was at once very busy – calling begins all over again after the seaside holiday, and she spent hours in the Buick saloon leaving cards. The voice was with her again, as before. But something had over-shadowed the blissful happiness of the spring days; there was an undertone of distress, of foreboding often, in the conversations. What exactly caused it she could not make out. But it increased, and one day half-way through October, driving in the East City, the voice dropped away into a burst of passionate sobbing. This distressed Mrs Bowlby extraordinarily. It was a strange and terrible thing to sit in the car with those low, heart-broken sounds at her side. She almost put out her arms to take and comfort the lovely unhappy creature – but there was only empty air, and the empty seat, with her bag, her book, and her little calling list. Obeying one of those sudden impulses which the voice alone seemed to call out in her, she abandoned her calls and told Shwang to drive to the Por Hua Shan Hut'ung. As they neared it the sobs beside her ceased, and murmured apologies for being *un peu énervée* followed.

When she reached the house Mrs Bowlby got out, and again climbed the ramp onto the Tartar Wall. The thorns and bushes between the battlements were brown and sere now, and no hoopoes flew and fluted among them. She reached the spot where she could look down into the garden. The lilacs were bare too, as her own were; the tubs of flowers were gone, and heaps of leaves had drifted round the feet of the acacias – only the white pine stood up, stately and untouched amid the general decay. A deep melancholy took hold of Mrs Bowlby; already shaken by the sobs in the car, the desolation of this deserted autumn garden weighed with an intense oppression on her spirit. She turned away slowly, and slowly descended to the Buick: The sense of impending misfortune had seized on her too; something, she vaguely felt, had come to an end in that garden.

As she was about to get into the car another impulse moved her. She felt an overmastering desire to enter the garden and see its features from close at hand. The oppression still hung over her, and she felt that a visit to the garden might in some way resolve it. She looked in her purse and found a five-dollar note. Handing it to the startled Shwang – 'Give that' said Mrs Bowlby, 'to the *k'ai-men-ti*, and tell him I wish to walk in the garden of that house.' Shwang bowed; rang the bell; conversed; Mrs Bowlby waited, trembling with impatience, till the clinching argument of the note was at last produced, and the old man whom she had seen before beckoned to her to enter.

She followed him through several courtyards. It was a rambling Chinese house, little modernised; the blind paper lattices of the windows looked blankly onto the miniature lakes and rocky landscapes in the open courts. Finally they passed through a round doorway into the garden below the Tartar Wall, and bowing, the old custodian stood aside to let her walk alone.

Before her rose the white pine, and she strolled towards it, and sitting down on a marble bench beside the round stone table, gazed about her. Beautiful even in its decay, melancholy, serene, the garden lay under the battlements which cut the pale autumn sky behind her. And here the owner of the voice had sat, hidden and secure, her lover beside her! A sudden burst of tears surprised Mrs Bowlby. Cruel Life, she thought, which parts dear lovers. Had *she* too sat here alone? A sharp unexpected sense of her own solitude drove Mrs Bowlby up from her seat. This visit was a mistake; her oppression was not lightened; to have sat in this place seemed somehow to have involved herself in the disaster and misery of that parted pair. She wandered on, through the fan-shaped doorway, and came to a halt beside the goldfish pond. Staring at it through her tears, she noticed the repair to the coping of which the voice had spoken, where Jacques had made an inscription in the damp mortar. She moved round to the place where it still showed white against the grey surface, murmuring, '*Maintenant il se lit là pour toujours, ton amour!*' – the phrase of the voice had stayed rooted in her mind. Stooping down, she read the inscription, scratched out neatly and carefully with a penknife in the fine plaster:

Douce sépulture, mon cœur dans ton cœur
Doux Paradis, mon âme dans ton âme.

And below two sets of initials:

A. DE A.
de
J. ST. G.B.B.

The verse touched Mrs Bowlby to fresh tears, and it was actually a moment or two before she focussed her attention on the initials. When she did, she started back, as though a serpent had stung her, and shut her eyes, and stood still. Then with a curious blind movement she opened her bag and took out one of her own cards, and laid it on the coping beside the inscription, as if to compare them. 'Mrs J. St. G.B. Bowlby' – the fine black letters stared up at her, uncompromising and clear, from the white oblong, beside the capitals cut in the plaster. There could be no mistake. Her mystery was solved at last, but it seemed as if she could not take it in. 'Jim?' murmured Mrs Bowlby to herself, as if puzzled – and then 'Jacques?' Slowly, while she stood there, all the connections and verifications unrolled themselves backwards in her mind with devastating certainty and force. Her sentiment, her intuition on the Wall had been terribly right – something *had* come to an end in that garden that day. Standing by the shamrock pond, with the first waves of an engulfing desolation sweeping over her, hardly conscious of her words, she whispered, '*Pourtant celà porte bonheur, le trèfle, n'est-ce pas?*'

And with that second quotation from the voice she seemed at last to wake from the sort of stupor in which she had stood. Intolerable! She must hear no more. Passing back, almost running, into the pine garden, she beckoned to the old *k'ai-men-ti* to take her out. He led her again, bowing, through the courtyards to the great gate-way. Through the open red-and-gold doors she saw the Buick saloon, dark and shiny, standing as she had so often, and with what pleasure, seen it stand before how many doors? She stopped and looked round her almost wildly – behind her the garden, before her the Buick. Liu caught sight of her, and flew to hold open the door. But Mrs Bowlby did not get in. She made Shwang call a ricksha, and when it came ordered him to direct the coolie to take her to the Bank. Shwang, exercising the respectful supervision which Chinese servants are wont to bestow on their employers, reminded her that she was to go to the polo to pick up the *lao-yé*, Bowlby. Before his astonished eyes his mistress shuddered visibly from head to foot. 'The Bank! The Bank!' she repeated, with a sort of desperate impatience.

Standing before his scarlet door, lighting his little black-and-silver pipe, the old *k'ai-men-ti* watched them go. First the ricksha, with a small drooping grey figure in it, lurched down the dusty *hu-t'ung*, and after it, empty, bumped the Buick saloon.

IX

In the Tube
E.F. Benson

From that excellent collection Visible and Invisible *by this author I have selected another little masterpiece set in the rather prosaic setting of the rush-hour tube. Having spent five years travelling to and from work on this mode of transportation I can testify to its speed and convenience, if not to its comfort. The Victoria Line, on which I was crushed and thrown about ten times a week, is one of the most modern of the Underground lines, but this story with its pre-war setting features some extinct stations that might puzzle modern readers. However tube haunting is tangible enough even today, although it is done mainly by lost Americans and unwashed guitar players in 1979.*

'It's a convention,' said Anthony Carling cheerfully, 'and not a very convincing one. Time, indeed! There's no such thing as Time really; it has no actual existence. Time is nothing more than an infinitesimal point in eternity, just as space is an infinitesimal point in infinity. At the most, Time is a sort of tunnel through which we are accustomed to believe that we are travelling. There's a roar in our ears and a darkness in our eyes which makes it seem real to us. But before we came into the tunnel we existed for ever in an infinite sunlight, and after we have got through it we shall exist in an infinite sunlight again. So why should we bother ourselves about the confusion and noise and darkness which only encompass us for a moment?'

For a firm-rooted believer in such immeasurable ideas as these, which he punctuated with brisk application of the poker to the brave sparkle and glow of the fire, Anthony has a very pleasant appreciation of the measurable and the finite, and nobody with whom I have acquaintance has so keen a zest for life and its enjoyments as he. He had given us this evening an admirable dinner, had passed round a port beyond praise, and had illuminated the jolly hours with the light of his infectious optimism. Now the small company had melted away, and I was left with him over the fire in his study. Outside the tattoo of wind-driven sleet was audible on the window-panes, over-scoring now and again the flap of the flames on the open hearth, and the thought of the chilly blasts and the snow-covered pavement in Brompton Square, across which, to skidding taxicabs, the last of his other guests had scurried, made my position, resident here till tomorrow morning, the more delicately delightful. Above all there was this stimulating and suggestive companion, who, whether he talked of the great abstractions which were so intensely real and practical to him, or of the very remarkable experiences which he had encountered among these conventions of time and space, was equally fascinating to the listener.

'I adore life,' he said. 'I find it the most entrancing plaything. It's a delightful game, and, as you know very well, the only conceivable way to play a game is to treat it extremely seriously. If you say to yourself, "It's only a game", you cease to take the slightest interest in it. You have to know that it's only a game and behave as if it was the one object of existence. I should like it to go on for many years yet. But all the time one has to be living on the true plane as well, which is eternity and infinity. If you come to think of it, the one thing which the human mind cannot grasp is the finite, not the infinite, the temporary, not the eternal.'

'That sounds rather paradoxical,' said I.

'Only because you've made a habit of thinking about things that seem bounded and limited. Look it in the face for a minute. Try to imagine finite Time and Space, and you find you can't. Go back a million years, and multiply that million of years by another million, and you find that you can't conceive of a beginning. What happened before that beginning? Another beginning and another beginning? And before that? Look at it like that, and you find that the only solution comprehensible to you is the existence of an eternity, something that never began and will never end. It's the same about space. Project yourself to the farthest star, and what comes beyond that? Emptiness? Go on through the emptiness, and you can't imagine it being finite and having an end. It must needs go on for ever: that's the only thing you can understand. There's no such thing as before or after, or beginning or end, and what a comfort that is! I should fidget myself to death if there wasn't the huge soft cushion of eternity to lean one's head against. Some people say – I believe I've heard you say it yourself – that the idea of eternity is so tiring; you felt that you want to stop. But that's because you are thinking of eternity in terms of Time, and mumbling in your brain, "And after that, and after that?" Don't you grasp the idea that in eternity there isn't any "after", any more than there is any "before"? It's all one. Eternity isn't a quantity: it's a quality.'

Sometimes, when Anthony talks in this manner, I seem to get a glimpse of that which to his mind is so transparently clear and solidly real, at other times (not having a brain that readily envisages abstractions) I feel as though he was pushing me over a precipice, and my intellectual faculties grasp wildly at anything tangible or comprehensible. This was the case now, and I hastily interrupted.

'But there is a "before" and "after",' I said. 'A few hours ago you gave us an admirable dinner, and after that – yes, after – we played bridge. And now you are going to explain things a little more clearly to me, and after that I shall go to bed – '

He laughed.

'You shall do exactly as you like,' he said, 'and you shan't be a slave to Time either tonight or tomorrow morning. We won't even mention an hour before breakfast, but you shall have it in eternity whenever you awake. And as I see it is not midnight yet, we'll slip the bonds of Time, and talk quite infinitely. I will stop the clock, if that will assist you in getting rid of your illusion, and then I'll tell you a story, which to my mind, shows how unreal so-called realities are; or, at any rate, how fallacious are our senses as judges of what is real and what is not.'

'Something occult, something spookish?' I asked, pricking up my ears, for Anthony has the strangest clairvoyances and visions of things unseen by the normal eye.

'I suppose you might call some of it occult,' he said, 'though there's a certain amount of rather grim reality mixed up in it.'

'Go on; excellent mixture,' said I.

He threw a fresh log on the fire.

'It's a longish story,' he said. 'You may stop me as soon as you've had enough. But there will come a point for which I claim your consideration. You, who cling to your "before" and "after", has it ever occurred to you how difficult it is to say *when* an incident takes place? Say that a man commits some crime of violence, can we not, with a good deal of truth, say that he really commits that crime when he definitely plans and determines upon it, dwelling on it with gusto? The actual commission of it, I think we can reasonably argue, is the mere material sequel of his resolve: he is guilty of it when he makes that determination. When, therefore, in the term of "before" and "after", does the crime truly take place? There is also in my story a further point for your consideration. For it seems certain that the spirit of a man, after the death of his body, is obliged to re-enact such a crime, with a view, I suppose we may guess, to his remorse and his eventual redemption. Those who have second sight have seen such re-enactments. Perhaps he may have done his deed blindly in this life; but then his spirit re-commits it with its spiritual eyes open, and able to comprehend its enormity. So, shall we view the man's original determination and the material commission of his crime only as preludes to the real commission of it, when with eyes unsealed he does it and repents of it? ... That all sounds very obscure when I speak in the abstract, but I think you will see what I mean, if you follow my tale. Comfortable? Got everything you want? Here goes, then.'

He leaned back in his chair, concentrating his mind, and then spoke:

'The story that I am about to tell you,' he said, 'had its beginning a month ago, when you were away in Switzerland. It reached its conclusion, so I imagine, last night. I do not, at any rate expect to experience any more of it. Well, a month ago I was returning late on a very wet night from dining out. There was not a taxi to be had, and I hurried through the pouring rain to the Tube-station at Piccadilly Circus, and thought myself very lucky to catch the last train in this direction. The carriage into which I stepped was quite empty except for one other passenger, who sat next the door immediately opposite to me. I had never, to my knowledge, seen him before, but I found my attention vividly fixed on him, as if he somehow concerned me. He was a man of middle age, in dress-clothes, and his face wore an expression of intense thought, as if in his mind he was pondering some very significant matter, and his hand which was resting on his knee clenched and unclenched itself. Suddenly he looked up and stared me in the face, and I saw there suspicion and fear, as if I had surprised him in some secret deed.

'At that moment we stopped at Dover Street, and the conductor threw open the doors, announced the station and added, "Change here for Hyde Park Corner and Gloucester Road". That was all right for me since it meant that the train would stop at Brompton Road, which was my destination. It was all right apparently, too, for my companion, for he certainly did not get out, and after a moment's stop, during which no one else got in, we went on. I saw him, I must insist, after the doors were closed and the train had started. But when I looked again, as we rattled on, I saw that there was no one there. I was quite alone in the carriage.

'Now you may think that I had had one of those swift momentary dreams which flash in and out of the mind in the space of a second, but I did not believe it was so myself, for I felt that I had experienced some sort of premonition or clairvoyant vision. A man, the semblance of whom, astral body or whatever you may choose to call it, I had just seen, would sometime sit in that seat opposite to me, pondering and planning.'

'But why?' I asked. 'Why should it have been the astral body of a living man which you thought you had seen? Why not the ghost of a dead one?'

'Because of my own sensations. The sight of the spirit of someone dead, which has occurred to me two or three times in my life, has always been accompanied by a physical shrinking and fear, and by the sensation of cold and loneliness. I believed, at any rate, that I had seen a phantom of the living, and that impression was confirmed, I might say proved, the next day. For I met the man himself. And the next night, as you shall hear, I met the phantom again. We will take them in order.

'I was lunching, then, the next day with my neighbour, Mrs Stanley; there was a small party, and when I arrived we waited but for the final guest. He entered while I was talking to some friend, and presently at my elbow I heard Mrs Stanley's voice –

' "Let me introduce you to Sir Henry Payle," she said.

'I turned and saw my *vis-à-vis* of the night before. It was quite unmistakably he, and as we shook hands he looked at me I thought with vague and puzzled recognition.

' "Haven't we met before, Mr Carling?" he said. "I seem to recollect – "

'For the moment I forgot the strange manner of his disappearance from the carriage, and thought that it had been the man himself whom I had seen last night.

' "Surely, and not so long ago," I said. "For we sat opposite each other in the last Tube-train from Piccadilly Circus yesterday night."

'He still looked at me, frowning, puzzled, and shook his head.

' "This can hardly be," he said. "I only came up from the country this morning."

'Now this interested me profoundly, for the astral body, we are told, abides in some half-conscious region of the mind or spirit, and has recollections of what has happened to it, which it can convey only very vaguely and dimly to the conscious mind. All lunch-time I could see his eyes again and again directed to me with the same puzzled and perplexed air, and as I was taking my departure he came up to me.

' "I shall recollect some day," he said, "where we met before, and I hope we may meet again. Was it not – ?" and he stopped. "No: it has gone from me," he added.'

The log that Anthony had thrown on the fire was burning bravely now, and its high-flickering flame lit up his face.

'Now, I don't know whether you believe in coincidences as chance things,' he said, 'but if you do, get rid of the notion. Or if you can't at once, call it a coincidence that that very night I again caught the last train on the Tube westwards. This time, so far from my being a solitary passenger, there was a considerable crowd waiting at Dover Street, where I entered, and just as the noise of the approaching train began to reverberate in the tunnel I caught sight of Sir Henry Payle standing near the opening from which the train would presently emerge, apart from the rest of the crowd. And I thought to myself how odd it was that I should have seen the phantom of him at this very hour last night and the man himself now, and I began walking towards him with the idea of saying, "Anyhow, it is in the Tube that we meet tonight" ... And then a terrible and awful thing happened. Just as the train emerged from the tunnel he jumped down on to the line in front of it, and the train swept along over him up the platform.

'For a moment I was stricken with horror at the sight, and I remember covering my eyes against the dreadful tragedy. But then I perceived that, though it had taken place in full sight of those who were waiting, no one seemed to have seen it except myself. The driver, looking out from his window, had not applied his brakes, there was no jolt from the advancing train, no scream, no cry, and the rest of the passengers began boarding the train with perfect nonchalance. I must have staggered, for I felt sick and faint with what I had seen, and some kindly soul put his arm round me and supported me into the train. He was a doctor, he told me, and asked if I was in pain, or what ailed me. I told him what I thought I had seen, and he assured me that no such accident had taken place.

'It was clear then to my own mind that I had seen the second act, so to speak, in this physical drama, and I pondered next morning over the problem as to what I should do. Already I had glanced at the morning paper, which, as I knew would be the case, contained no mention whatever of what I had seen. The thing had certainly not happened, but I knew in myself that it would happen. The flimsy veil of Time had been withdrawn from my eyes, and I had seen into what you would call the future. In terms of Time of course it was the future, but from my point of view the thing was just as much in the past as it was in the future. It existed, and waited only for its material fulfilment. The more I thought about it, the more I saw that I could do nothing.'

I interrupted his narrative.

'You did nothing?' I exclaimed. 'Surely you might have taken some step in order to avert the tragedy.'

He shook his head.

'What step precisely?' he said. 'Was it to go to Sir Henry and tell him that once more I had seen him in the Tube in the act of committing suicide? Look at it like this. Either what I had seen was pure illusion, pure imagination, in which case it had no existence or significance at all, or it was actual and real, and essentially it had happened. Or take it, though not very logically, somewhere between the two. Say that the idea of suicide, for some cause of which I knew nothing, had occurred to him or would occur. Should I not, if that was the case, be doing a very dangerous thing, by making such a suggestion to him? Might not the fact of my telling him what I had seen put the idea into his mind, or, if it was already there, confirm it and strengthen it? "It's a ticklish matter to play with souls," as Browning says.'

'But it seems so inhuman not to interfere in any way,' said I, 'not to make an attempt.'

'What interference?' asked he. 'What attempt?'

The human interest in me still seemed to cry aloud at the thought of doing nothing to avert such a tragedy, but it seemed to be beating itself against something austere and inexorable. And cudgel my brain as I would, I could not combat the sense of what he had said. I had no answer for him, and he went on.

'You must recollect, too,' he said, 'that I believed then and believe now that the thing had happened. The cause of it, whatever that was, had begun to work, and the effect, in this material sphere, was inevitable. That is what I alluded to when, at the beginning of my story, I asked you to consider how difficult it was to say when an action took place. You still hold that this particular action, this suicide of Sir Henry, had not yet taken place, because he had not yet thrown himself under the advancing train. To me that seems a materialistic view. I hold that in all but the endorsement of it, so to speak, it had taken place. I fancy that Sir Henry, for instance, now free from the material dusks, knows that himself.'

Exactly as he spoke there swept through the warm lit room

a current of ice-cold air, ruffling my hair as it passed me, and making the wood flames on the hearth to dwindle and flare. I looked round to see if the door at my back had opened, but nothing stirred there, and over the closed window the curtains were fully drawn. As it reached Anthony, he sat up quickly in his chair and directed his glance this way and that about the room.

'Did you feel that?' he asked.

'Yes: a sudden draught,' I said. 'Ice-cold.'

'Anything else?' he asked. 'Any other sensation?'

I paused before I answered, for at the moment there occurred to me Anthony's differentiation of the effects produced on the beholder by a phantasm of the living and the apparition of the dead. It was the latter which accurately described my sensations now, a certain physical shrinking, a fear, a feeling of desolation. But yet I had seen nothing. 'I felt rather creepy,' I said.

As I spoke I drew my chair rather closer to the fire, and sent a swift and, I confess, a somewhat apprehensive scrutiny round the walls of the brightly lit room. I noticed at the same time that Anthony was peering across to the chimney-piece, on which, just below a sconce holding two electric lights, stood the clock which at the beginning of our talk he had offered to stop. The hands I noticed pointed to twenty-five minutes to one.

'But you saw nothing?' he asked.

'Nothing whatever,' I said. 'Why should I? What was there to see? Or did you – '

'I don't think so,' he said.

Somehow this answer got on my nerves, for the queer feeling which had accompanied that cold current of air had not left me. If anything it had become more acute.

'But surely you know whether you saw anything or not?' I said.

'One can't always be certain,' said he. 'I say that I don't think I saw anything. But I'm not sure, either, whether the story I am telling you was quite concluded last night. I think there may be a further incident. If you prefer it, I will leave the rest of it, as far as I know it, unfinished till tomorrow morning, and you can go off to bed now.'

His complete calmness and tranquillity reassured me.

'But why should I do that?' I asked.

Again he looked round on the bright walls.

'Well, I think something entered the room just now,' he said, 'and it may develop. If you don't like the notion, you had better go. Of course there's nothing to be alarmed at; whatever it is, it can't hurt us. But it is close on the hour when on two successive nights I saw what I have already told you, and an apparition usually occurs at the same time. Why that is so, I cannot say, but certainly it looks as if a spirit that is earth-bound is still subject to certain conventions, the conventions of time for instance. I think that personally I shall see something before long, but most likely you won't. You're not such a sufferer as I from these – these delusions – '

I was frightened and knew it, but I was also intensely interested, and some perverse pride wriggled within me at his last words. Why, so I asked myself, shouldn't I see whatever was to be seen ...?

'I don't want to go in the least,' I said. 'I want to hear the rest of your story.'

'Where was I, then? Ah, yes: you were wondering why I didn't do something after I saw the train move up to the platform, and I said that there was nothing to be done. If you think it over, I fancy you will agree with me ... A couple of days passed, and on the third morning I saw in the paper that there had come fulfilment to my vision. Sir Henry Payle, who had been waiting on the platform of Dover Street Station for the last train to South Kensington, had thrown himself in front of it as it came to the station. The train had been pulled up in a couple of yards, but a wheel had passed over his chest, crushing it in and instantly killing him.

'An inquest was held, and there emerged at it one of those dark stories which, on occasions like these, sometimes fall like a midnight shadow across a life that the world perhaps had thought prosperous. He had long been on bad terms with his wife, from whom he had lived apart, and it appeared that not long before this he had fallen desperately in love with another woman. The night before his suicide he had appeared very late at his wife's house, and had a long and angry scene with her in which he entreated her to divorce him, threatening otherwise to make her life a hell to her. She refused, and in an ungovernable fit of passion he attempted to strangle her. There was a struggle, and the noise of it caused her manservant to come up, who succeeded in overmastering him. Lady Payle threatened to proceed against him for assault with the intention to murder her. With this hanging over his head, the next night, as I have already told you, he committed suicide.'

He glanced at the clock again, and I saw that the hands now pointed to ten minutes to one. The fire was beginning to burn low and the room surely was growing strangely cold.

'That's not quite all,' said Anthony, again looking round. 'Are you sure you wouldn't prefer to hear it tomorrow?'

The mixture of shame and pride and curiosity again prevailed.

'No: tell me the rest of it at once,' I said.

Before speaking, he peered suddenly at some point behind my chair, shading his eyes. I followed his glance, and knew what he meant by saying that sometimes one could not be sure whether one saw something or not. But was that an outlined shadow that intervened between me and the wall? It was difficult to focus; I did not know whether it was near the wall or near my chair. It seemed to clear away, anyhow, as I looked more closely at it.

'You see nothing?' asked Anthony.

'No: I don't think so,' said I. 'And you?'

'I think I do,' he said, and his eyes followed something which was invisible to mine. They came to rest between him and the chimney-piece. Looking steadily there, he spoke again.

'All this happened some weeks ago,' he said, 'when you were out in Switzerland, and since then, up till last night, I saw nothing further. But all the time I was expecting something further. I felt that, as far as I was concerned, it was not all over yet, and last night, with the intention of assisting any communication to come through to me from – from beyond, I went into the Dover Street Tube-station at a few minutes before one o'clock, the hour at which both the assault and the suicide had taken place. The platform when I arrived on it was absolutely empty, or appeared to be so, but

presently, just as I began to hear the roar of the approaching
train, I saw there was the figure of a man standing some
twenty yards from me, looking into the tunnel. He had not
come down with me in the lift, and the moment before he had
not been there. He began moving towards me, and then I saw
who it was, and I felt a stir of wind icy-cold coming towards
me as he approached. It was not the draught that heralds the
approach of a train, for it came from the opposite direction.
He came close up to me, and I saw there was recognition in his
eyes. He raised his face towards me and I saw his lips move,
but, perhaps in the increasing noise from the tunnel, I heard
nothing come from them. He put out his hand, as if entreating
me to do something, and with a cowardice from which I
cannot forgive myself, I shrank from him, for I knew, by the
sign that I have told you, that this was one from the dead, and
my flesh quaked before him, drowning for the moment all pity
and all desire to help him, if that was possible. Certainly he
had something which he wanted of me, but I recoiled from
him. And by now the train was emerging from the tunnel, and
next moment, with a dreadful gesture of despair, he threw
himself in front of it.'

As he finished speaking he got up quickly from his chair,
still looking fixedly in front of him. I saw his pupils dilate, and
his mouth worked.

'It is coming,' he said. 'I am to be given a chance of atoning
for my cowardice. There is nothing to be afraid of: I must
remember that myself ...'

As he spoke there came from the panelling above the
chimney-piece one loud shattering crack, and the cold wind
again circled about my head. I found myself shrinking back in
my chair with my hands held in front of me as instinctively I
screened myself against something which I knew was there
but which I could not see. Every sense told me that there was a
presence in the room other than mine and Anthony's and the
horror of it was that I could not see it. Any vision, however
terrible, would, I felt, be more tolerable than this clear certain
knowledge that close to me was this invisible thing. And yet
what horror might not be disclosed of the face of the dead and
the crushed chest ... But all I could see, as I shuddered in this
cold wind, was the familiar walls of the room, and Anthony

standing in front of me stiff and firm, making, as I knew, a call on his courage. His eyes were focused on something quite close to him, and some semblance of a smile quivered on his mouth. And then he spoke again.

'Yes, I know you,' he said. 'And you want something of me. Tell me, then, what it is.'

There was absolute silence, but what was silence to my ears could not have been to his, for once or twice he nodded, and once he said, 'Yes: I see. I will do it.' And with the knowledge that, even as there was someone here whom I could not see, so there was speech going on which I could not hear, this terror of the dead and of the unknown rose in me with the sense of powerlessness to move that accompanies nightmare. I could not stir, I could not speak. I could only strain my ears for the inaudible and my eyes for the unseen, while the cold wind from the very valley of the shadow of death streamed over me. It was not that the presence of death itself was terrible; it was that from its tranquillity and serene keeping there had been driven some unquiet soul unable to rest in peace for whatever ultimate awakening rouses the countless generations of those who have passed away, driven, no less, from whatever activities are theirs, back into the material world from which it should have been delivered. Never, until the gulf between the living and the dead was thus bridged, had it seemed so immense and so unnatural. It is possible that the dead may have communication with the living, and it was not that exactly that so terrified me, for such communication, as we know it, comes voluntarily from them. But here was something icy-cold and crime-laden, that was chased back from the peace that would not pacify it.

And then, most horrible of all, there came a change in these unseen conditions. Anthony was silent now, and from looking straight and fixedly in front of him, he began to glance sideways to where I sat and back again, and with that I felt that the unseen presence had turned its attention from him to me. And now, too, gradually and by awful degrees I began to see ...

There came an outline of shadow across the chimney-piece and the panels above it. It took shape: it fashioned itself into the outline of a man. Within the shape of the shadow details

began to form themselves, and I saw wavering in the air, like
something concealed by haze, the semblance of a face, stricken
and tragic, and burdened with such a weight of woe as no
human face had ever worn. Next, the shoulders outlined
themselves, and a stain livid and red spread out below them,
and suddenly the vision leaped into clearness. There he stood,
the chest crushed in and drowned in the red stain, from which
broken ribs, like the bones of a wrecked ship, protruded. The
mournful, terrible eyes were fixed on me, and it was from
them, so I knew, that the bitter wind proceeded ...

Then, quick as the switching off of a lamp, the spectre
vanished, and the bitter wind was still, and opposite to me
stood Anthony, in a quiet, bright-lit room. There was no sense
of an unseen presence any more; he and I were then alone,
with an interrupted conversation still dangling between us in
the warm air. I came round to that, as one comes round after
an anaesthetic. It all swam into sight again, unreal at first,
and gradually assuming the texture of actuality.

'You were talking to somebody, not to me,' I said. 'Who
was it? What was it?'

He passed the back of his hand over his forehead, which
glistened in the light.

'A soul in hell,' he said.

Now it is hard ever to recall mere physical sensations, when
they have passed. If you have been cold and are warmed, it is
difficult to remember what cold was like; if you have been hot
and have got cool, it is difficult to realize what the oppression
of heat really meant. Just so, with the passing of that presence,
I found myself unable to recapture the sense of the terror with
which, a few moments ago only, it had invaded and inspired
me.

'A soul in hell?' I said. 'What are you talking about?'

He moved about the room for a minute or so, and then came
and sat on the arm of my chair.

'I don't know what you saw,' he said, 'or what you felt, but
there has never in all my life happened to me anything more
real than what these last few minutes have brought. I have
talked to a soul in the hell of remorse, which is the only
possible hell. He knew, from what happened last night, that
he could perhaps establish communication through me with

the world he had quitted, and he sought me and found me. I am charged with a mission to a woman I have never seen, a message from the contrite ... You can guess who it is ...'

He got up with a sudden briskness.

'Let's verify it anyhow,' he said. 'He gave me the street and the number. Ah, there's the telephone book! Would it be a coincidence merely if I found that at No 20 in Chasemore Street, South Kensington, there lived a Lady Payle?'

He turned over the leaves of the bulky volume.

'Yes, that's right,' he said.

X

The Attic Express
Alex Hamilton

If men love cars, then they adore trains, at least when they are young. But men never grow up in that respect, women claim. With model trains the excuse that one is helping the children with it has carried many a father through an enjoyable day, and what could be safer or more harmless than such a hobby? Provided of course that one does not carry the realism to fatal extremes.

In the evenings they climbed the steep narrow stairway to the big room under the roof. Hector Coley went up eagerly and alertly. The boy followed his father draggingly. In the family it had always been called 'Brian's room', but to Brian it seemed that his father's presence filled it.

It was a long room, with low sidewalls and a ceiling like the lower half of an A. There was a large water-tank at one end: the rest of the space was 'Brian's'.

Coley ran the trains. The boy looked on.

Sometimes, when his father was absorbed, attending to midget couplings, rearranging a length of track, wiring up a tiny house so that it could be lit from inside, he looked away, and merely watched the single square of attic window gently darken.

Coley hated Brian to lose interest. He would say irritably: 'I can't understand you, Brian, beggared if I can! You know something? Some boys would give an arm to have the run of a playroom like this one I've built for you.'

The boy would shift his gaze and rub his hands together nervously. He would stoop forward hastily and peer at all parts of the track. 'Make it go through the crossing,' he would say, to appease his father. But even before the magnificent little Fleischmann engine challenged the gradient to the crossing – which would involve the delicious manoeuvre of braking two or three small cars – his eye would be away again, after a moth on the wall, or a cloud veiling the moon.

'It defeats me,' Coley would say later to his wife, 'he shows no interest in anything. Sometimes I don't get a word out of him all evening unless I drag it out of him.'

'Perhaps he's not old enough yet,' she would reply diffidently, 'you know I think I'd find it a little difficult to manage myself – all those signals and control switches and lights going on and off and trains going this way and that way. I'm glad I'm never asked to work out anything more complicated than a Fair Isle knitting pattern.'

'You miss the point,' said Coley impatiently, 'I'm not expecting him to synchronize the running times of ten trains, and keep them all safely on the move, but I would like a spark of enthusiasm to show now and again, I mean, I give up hours of my time, not to speak of money running into thousands, to give him a lay-out which I'm willing to wager a couple of bob can't be matched in any home in Britain, and he can't even do me the courtesy of listening to me when I explain something. It's not good enough.'

'I know, dear, how you feel, but at ten I do feel it's a little ...'

'Oh, rubbish,' exclaimed Coley, 'ten's a helluvan age. At ten I could dismantle a good watch and put it together again better than new.'

'You are exceptional, dear. Not everyone has your mechanical bent. I expect Brian's will show itself in time.'

'There again, will it? His reports all read the same: "Could do much better if he applied himself more ... doesn't get his teeth into it ..." and so on till I could give him a jolly good hiding. No, Meg, say what you like, it's plain to me that the boy simply won't try.'

'In some subjects he's probably a little better than in others.'

'Nonsense,' said Coley energetically, 'anybody can do anything, if they want to enough.'

One evening, after listening to his complaints meekly for a while, she suddenly interrupted him:

'Where is he now?'

'Where I left him. I've given him the new express in its box. I want to see whether he's got enough gumption to set it out on the track with the right load. If I find it's still in the box when I get back ...'

'Yes, dear,' she said, surprising him with her vehemence, 'why don't you bring the matter to a head? It's getting on my nerves a bit, you know, sitting down here reading and watching television, and imagining you struggling. If he's not really interested, then could we have an end to all this? I know the railways are your pride, but honestly I'd rather see them scrapped than listen to any more of this.'

He was astonished. He went back upstairs without a word.

The boy was squatting, with his face cupped in one hand, elbow on knee. His straight brown hair fell forward and half obscured his face. The other arm dangled loosely, and the forefinger of his hand moved an empty light truck to and fro a few inches on the floor.

The express was on the rails. Brian had it at the head of an extraordinarily miscellaneous collection of waggons: Pullmans, goods trucks, restaurant cars, breakdown waggons, timber trucks, oil canisters – anything, obviously, which had come to hand.

'Sit down at the control panel, Brian,' snapped Coley.

The boy did not reply, but he did what he was told.

'I want you to run this express tonight,' said Coley, 'and I'm not going to lift a finger to help. But I'll be fair, too, I won't criticize. I'll stay right out of it. In fact for all you know I might as well be on the train itself. Think of me being on it, that's it, and run it accordingly ...'

He was trying to keep the anger and disappointment out of his voice. The boy half turned a moment, and looked at him steadily, then he resumed his scrutiny of the control panel.

'... take your time ... think it all out ... don't do anything hastily ... keep your wits about you ... remember all I've taught you ... that's a gorgeous little model I've got there for you ... I'm on board ... up on the footplate if you like ... we'll have a gala and just have it lit with the illuminations of the set itself ... give me time to get aboard ... I'm in your hands, son ...'

Coley stood on the railway line. The giant express faced him, quiet, just off the main line. He started to walk along the track towards it.

He felt no astonishment at finding himself in scale with the models. *Anyone can do anything, if they want to enough.* He'd wished to drive a model, from the footplate, and here he was walking towards it.

But at the first step he took, he sank up to his knees in the ballast below the track. It was, after all, only foam rubber. He grinned. 'I'll have to remember things like that,' he told himself.

He stopped by the engine and looked up at the boiler. He whistled softly between his teeth, excited by so much beauty. What a lovely job these Germans made of anything they tackled. Not a plate out of line. A really sumptuous, genuine, top of the form job! He wished the maker a ton of good dinners. The thing was real, not a doubt.

He stepped on through tiny, incisive pebbles of sand, treading cautiously. One or two had threatened to cut into his shoes. Looking down, he noticed a right-angled bar of metal, gleaming at his feet. He realized in a moment that it must be one of the staples which had held the engine's box together. Chuckling over his own drollness at playing the game to the full, he picked up the bar and with an effort almost succeeded in straightening it right out. Then he advanced on the wheel and tapped it. The wheel was, of course, sound. He ran his hand over the virgin wheel. He lifted his arm and placed his hand against the smooth gloss of the boiler. He could do that because it was quite cold. He smiled again: that took away a bit of the realism, to think of a steam engine run on electricity. When you were down to scale, it seemed you noticed these things.

Then he frowned as he noticed something else. The coupling of the first carriage, a Pullman, could not have been properly made up by Brian. The first wheels were well clear of the rails. He ran past the tender to have a look. Sure enough. Damn careless of him! He was about to call out to Brian, when he remembered his promise to say nothing, and thought he'd make the correction himself. It was just a matter of sliding the arm across until the spoke fell into the slot in the rear of the tender. The remainder of the fastening was simple. He jabbed the lever in under the arm and strained to shift the carriage.

After a minute, during which the carriage swayed a bit but did not move, he stopped and took off his coat. He was still in his office suit. He wished he were in his old flannels and lumberjack shirt, but at least he hadn't changed into slippers. Sweat trickled down his back. He hadn't had much time for exercise lately, though his usual practice was conditioning on the links, alternate fifteen yards running and walking, for eighteen holes. Without clubs, of course.

He hurled himself at it again, bracing his full weight against the lever. Suddenly the arm shifted, and skidded over the new surface on which it rested. The spoke found the slot, and the whole carriage crashed into position on the rails. The lever flicked off with rending force, and one spinning end struck him under the arm, just near the shoulder.

He thought he would be sick with the pain. All feeling went out of his arm, except at the point of impact. There was plenty of feeling, all vividly unpleasant. Almost mechanically he leant down and picked up his jacket. Trailing it, he tottered back to the engine, and slowly hoisted himself into the cab. There he leant over one of the immobile levers until he had partially recovered.

He was still palpating his startled flesh, and establishing that no bones was broken, when, without any preliminary warning, the train suddenly jerked into motion. Wheeling round, he managed to save himself from falling by hooking himself into the window of the cab. He looked for his son, to signal that he was not quite ready yet. Even without the blow he had just sustained he would have liked a few more minutes to adjust himself to the idea of being part of a model world, before the journey began.

But he couldn't at first see where he was. In this fantastic landscape, lit but not warmed by three suns, all the familiar features had undergone a change. The sensation resembled in some way that which comes to a man who visits a district he knows well by daylight, for the first time after dark.

In the direct light of those three suns, an overhead monster and two wall brackets, everything glittered. Plain to Coley, but less noticeable to the boy at the table on which was spread the control panel, were separate shadows of differing intensity radiating from every upright object. But the objects themselves sparkled. Light came flashing and twinkling and glancing from the walls and roofs of the houses, from the foliage of the trees, from the heaps of coal by the sidings, from the clothes and faces of the men and women. The lines of the railway themselves shone, twisting and turning a hundred times amongst windmills and farms and garages and fields and stations, all throwing back this aggressive, stupefying brilliance of light. Coley screwed up his eyes and tried to work it out. The train slipped forward smoothly, gaining momentum. The boy hadn't made a bad job of the start, anyway. Perhaps he took in more than I imagined, said Coley to himself.

He fixed his eye on a vast grey expanse, stretching away parallel to the course they were on, and appearing like a long rectangular field of some kind of close undergrowth with curling tops. What the devil could that be? He didn't remember putting down anything like that. Whatever it was, it didn't look anything like the real thing, now that he was down to scale. A breeze stirred small clumps which seemed to ride clear of the rest, and it came to him that, of course, this was the strip of carpet he'd laid down on one side of the room, always insisting that people should walk only on this if possible, to prevent breakages.

If that was the carpet ... he rushed across to the other window, just in time before the engine started to take a corner, to see the top of his son's head, bent over the controls.

It was miles away! So huge! So ... dare he admit it to himself ... grotesque! The line of his parting, running white across his scalp, showed to the man in the cab like a streak in a forest, a blaze consequent upon roadmaking. A house could have been hidden behind the hair falling across his forehead. The shadow of his son on the burning white sky behind was like a storm cloud.

Brian disappeared from his view as the track curled, and Coley shook his head, as if he could clear away these images as a dog rattles away drops of water from its fur. 'It's not like me to imagine things,' said Coley fiercely. All the same, drops of moisture stood out on the back of the hand which clutched a lever.

He sensed a slight acceleration. The telegraph poles were coming by now at more than one a second. He felt the use of his injured arm returning, and with it a return of self-confidence. 'I wonder if, when I return to my normal size, the bruise will be to scale or be only, quite literally, a scratch?'

He was about to resume his jacket, since the wind was now considerable, when the train turned again and he lost his balance. In falling, the jacket fell from his hand, and was whipped away out of the cab.

Unhurt by his fall, but irritated by the loss of the jacket, Coley pulled himself to his feet and swore: 'Hell of a lot of bends on this railway,' as if he were perceiving it for the first time, 'anyway, that doesn't matter so much, I can put up with a fresh wind for a while if he'd only think what all this bloody light is doing to my eyes. Tone down the ruddy glare, can't you?'

As if in answer, the suns were extinguished.

For an instant the succeeding blackness was complete.

The express forged almost noiselessly through the dark. Coley fumbled for handholds. 'That's a bit inefficient,' he muttered. But the totality of darkness was not for long. Simultaneously, and Coley imagined Brian studying the switches, all the lights in the houses and stations and farms and windmills, and so forth, were flipped on.

'That's really rather nice to look at!' said Coley, appreciatively. 'I always knew I'd done a good job there, but it's only now that I can see just how good. I don't think they can complain there,' he went on. 'I think they'd admit I've looked after that little creature comfort.' He was referring to the little people with whom he had populated the world in which the attic express was running.

He also thought, as the walls of the attic vanished altogether: 'If he hasn't noticed that the old man's no longer sitting in the armchair behind him, he's not likely to now. It would be rather good to slip back into the chair before the lights go up again. I'll have to watch my moment as soon as he's had enough and stops the express.'

They sped through a crossing. Coley, looking down on it,

and at the figures massed by the gate, observed a solitary figure in a patch of light, waving. Whimsically, he waved back. The expression on the face of the waving man was one of jubilation. His smile reached, literally, from ear to ear. 'A cheery chappie,' remarked Coley. He was beginning to enjoy himself.

At a comfortable pace the express swung into the long straight which led into the area described on the posters and signboards as Coleyville. It was the largest and best equipped of the five stations. Coley thought that Brian must see it as an inevitable stop. Interesting to see whether he could bring it in to a nice easy check. The passengers might be assumed to be taking down their suitcases, and dragging on their coats, and would be resentful at being overbalanced.

Far up ahead Coley could see the platform approaching. He could make out the long line of people waiting to climb aboard. A representative body of folk, thought Coley, I got in a good cross-section of the travelling public for Coleyville. Then, flashing down the hill, on the road which would cross the track just this side of the station in a scissors intersection, Coley saw an open sports car. It was coming down at a frightening speed, and should reach the junction just as the express went through.

'The young monkey!' breathed Coley, 'he must be getting into the swing of it.' For a moment he tensed, until he remembered that on this crossing there was a synchronization which would automatically brake the car. A high, whining metallic noise filled his ears from the single rail of the roadster, which abruptly cut off as the car was stopped.

'From eighty to rest in a split second,' thought Coley, 'that's not too realistic. Not the boy's fault, but I'll have to see if I can't improve on that.' He also noticed, as the express moved slowly through the crossing, that there were no features on the face of the roadster's driver. Not even eyes! 'No use telling you to look where you're going!' shouted Coley. The square-shouldered driver sat upright and motionless, waiting for the express to be out of his way.

The express stopped at Coleyville.

'Perfect!' exclaimed Coley, 'just perfect!' He wished he could shake Brian's hand. The boy must care after all, to be able to handle the stuff in this way. His heart swelled. He thought for a moment of stepping off at Coleyville and watching from the outside for a while, and then pick her up again next time she stopped. But he couldn't be sure the boy would bring her round again on the same line. And this was far too exhilarating an adventure to duck out of now. He stayed.

He leant out of the cab and looked down the platform at the people waiting. It was a mild surprise to him that no one moved. There they stood, their baggage in their hands or at their feet, waiting for trains, and doing nothing about it when one came. He saw the guard, staring at him. The guard's face was a violent maroon colour, and the front part of one foot was missing. He had doubtless good reasons for drinking heavily. Immediately behind him was a lovely blonde, about seven feet high, and with one breast considerably larger than the other, but otherwise delicious to look at. At her side was a small boy in suit and school cap. He had the face of a middle-aged man. Farther on down a toothless mastiff gambolled, at the end of a leash held by a gentleman in city suit and homburg. He was flawless, but for the fact that he had omitted to put on collar and tie.

Coley rubbed the side of his nose with his index finger. 'I never expected to discover that you had such curious characters,' he said ruefully. The guard stared at him balefully, the blonde proudly. The express moved out of the station. Coley took his shoe off and hammered the glass out of the right-hand foreport. It was too opaque for proper vision. He smiled as he thought of the faces of the makers if he should write to them criticizing. Being Germans, they'd take it seriously, and put the matter right in future.

Beyond Coleyville the track wound through low hills. Coleyville was a dormitory town, but on the outskirts were some prosperous farms whose flocks could be seen all about the hills. A well-appointed country club lay at the foot of the high land which bordered the east wall, which was continued in illusion by a massive photograph of the Pennines which Coley had had blown up to extend most of the length of the wall. It was, in Coley's view, one of the most agreeable and meticulously arranged districts in his entire lay-out.

By the fences of the farms stood children, waving. Yokels waved. Lambs and dogs frisked. A water-mill turned slowly. It ran on a battery, but looked very real. Plump milkmaids meandered to and fro. 'Lovely spot for a holiday,' thought urban Coley, sentimentally. He leant far out of the cab window to have a better view of the whole wide perspective, and almost had his head taken off by a passing goods train.

It came up very softly, passing on the outside of a curve. Coley withdrew his head only because he happened to catch a slight shadow approach.

He leant his face against the cold metal by his window.

'Idiot!' he said to himself in fright and anger.

The goods train went by at a smart clip. There were only about five trucks on it, all empty.

'Steady, old chap!' he apostrophized his son, under his breath, 'don't take on too much all at once.'

For the first time it occurred to him that it might be a good thing to be ready to skip clear in the event of danger. Brian was operating very sensibly at present, but a lapse in concentration ... A vague chill passed down Coley's spine.

He looked back at the train on which he was travelling. It might be better to pick his way to the rear coaches.

He took three strides and launched himself on to the tender, Landing, he tore his trousers on the rough surface which represented coal nuts. It was very slippery and he almost slid right over it altogether, but he contrived to dig toes and hands into the depressions and check himself.

The express was moving along an embankment. Below him he could see the figures of young women in bathing suits disporting themselves about a glass swimming pool. Uniformed waiters stood obsequiously about, handing drinks to shirt-sleeved gentlemen under beach umbrellas. In the context of night-time the scene appeared macabre and hinting of recondite pleasures, particularly when the white legs of one of the beauties, protruding from under a glistering, russet bush, were taken into account. She could have been a corpse, and none of the high-lifers caring.

Coley wriggled forward cautiously over the hard black lumps. He wished now he'd stayed where he was, since the strong wind was more than he had allowed for.

He scrambled to a sitting position on the hard, pointed surface of the tender. Beyond the country club, looking ahead, were the mountains. He sought about for the secure footholds he'd need before making his leap off the tender into the gaping doorway of the Pullman behind, but decided to postpone the effort until the express had passed through the long tunnel. There was a long gentle declivity on the far side, a gradient of 1/248 he'd posted it, and he'd have a more stable vehicle to jump to. Besides, in the tunnel it would be dark.

He remembered himself one Sunday morning, making the mountain secure above the tunnel. The trouble he'd had with that material, nailing it in firmly without damaging any of the features of the landscape built on to it.

Those nails!

Some must protrude into the tunnel itself! He'd never troubled himself about them. There had always been plenty of clearance for the trains themselves. But, for him, perched on top of the tender? He looked round desperately to see if he might still have time to make his leap.

But he had remembered too late. The tunnel sucked them in like a mouth. He rolled flat on his face and prayed.

It was not completely dark, though very nearly so. A vague glow came through at one section where a tricky bit of building had been finally effected with painted canvas, and in it he was lucky to spot one of the nails and wriggle clear. The other he never saw. The point, aimed perpendicularly downwards, just caught his collar, as it arched upward over his straining neck.

He was jerked up bodily. It was very swift. He had no time to do anything about it. For a second he seemed to be suspended on the very tip of the nail, then the shirt tore and he was delivered back on the train.

He landed with a vicious thump on some part of a waggon some distance below roof-level. Something drove like the tip of a boot into his knee and he doubled over against what might be a rail. He clung to it. He couldn't tell where he was, but he could hear a wheel clicking furiously beneath him. Gasping from the pain of his knee, and a dull throb between the shoulder blades, he hung on and waited for the end of the tunnel and light.

It came suddenly.

His first feeling was relief that he had been thrown almost on the very spot he had chosen to jump to before the train entered the tunnel. But this was succeeded by a stab of anguish from his back as he raised himself to his feet in the doorway of the Pullman. He put his hand behind his back and found first that his shirt had split all the way to his trousers. He allowed it to flow down his arms, and held it in one hand while he probed his back with the other.

'Ye Gods,' he murmured shakily as he examined his hand after feeling his wound, 'I must be bleeding like a stuck pig!'

Slowly he converted his shirt into a great bandage, wrapping it around his chest, under his armpits and tying it below his chin, like a bra in reverse. While he was doing this, grunting as much from astonishment at his predicament as from pain, the express accelerated, and as it thundered along the decline his horror at this was added to the confusion of his feelings.

'I must stop this,' he said thickly, 'I must signal the boy to cut the power off.' He reeled into the Pullman. On the far side he seemed to remember there was a flat truck with nothing on it but a couple of logs. Perhaps if he got astride one of them, he could make himself be seen.

From nowhere appeared the colossal torso of a man. It was white coated, but the face was mottled, a sort of piebald, with only one deeply sunken eye, and the other the faintest smear at the point of the normal cheekbone.

'Get away! Get away!' screamed Coley, striking out at it wildly. One of his blows landed high on the man's chest. He teetered a moment, and then, without bending, went over on his back. The material from which he was made was very light. He was no more than amalgam of plastics and painted hat.

Coley looked down at the prostrate dummy and rubbed his bloodied hand over his forehead. 'No sense in getting hysterical,' he warned himself. He stepped over the prostrate figure, twisting to avoid the outstretched arm. He observed with revulsion that the fingers on the hand were webbed, a glittering duck-egg blue. Coley ran his tongue over his lips, tasting blood. 'Take a brace,' he admonished himself, reverting to the slang of his schooldays, 'don't let your imagination run away with you.'

He staggered amongst the conclaves of seated gentlemen, for ever impassive and at their ease in armchairs, content with the society in which they found themselves, unimpressed by the increasing momentum of the express, welded to their very chairs. Coley shot a glance over the gleaming carapace of one stern hock-drinker and out through the window. The variety of the landscape was flickering by with alarming speed, becoming a gale of altering colours. The coach was beginning to sway.

Coley broke into a run. The roar below him apprised him that the express was travelling over the suspension bridge. The bridge had been his pride, a labour of months, not bought whole, but built from wire and plywood in his leisure hours. He had no time now for gloating.

'I must get him to see me, or I'm done for.'

But beyond the Pullman, he found another waggon, a restaurant car. In his haste he had forgotten that one. He dashed down the aisle, grabbing tables to steady himself against the rocking of the train as he went. They must be up to seventy now, or rather about four miles an hour, he realized with bitterness.

Leaning a moment over one of the tables, he saw that the lamps in the centre were bulky, heavy-looking objects. He heaved tentatively at one of them, and it snapped off at the base. The diners, with their hands in their laps, stared on across the table at each other, untroubled by the onslaught of this wild-eyed Englishman. The Englishman, naked to the waist, his shirt sleeves dangling red and filthy down his chest, his body flaming now with a dozen bruises, stood over them a second clutching the lamp to him, panting heavily, then turned away and reeled on down the aisle. Down his retreating back the blood was flowing now freely. The shirt was inadequate to check it as it escaped from the savage wound he had sustained in the tunnel.

This time when he emerged at the doorway of the carriage he found himself looking at the open truck on which were chained four logs. He flung the lampstand ahead of him and it landed satisfyingly between two of the logs. He gathered his ebbing strength for the jump.

He was just able to make it. He caught his foot in one of the chains in mid-flight and crashed down on his face, but he saved himself from disaster by flinging one arm round a log. He sat up immediately and looked about him.

For a moment his vision was partly blocked as yet another train flashed by in the opposite direction. 'Oh, God, what's he playing at?' whispered Coley, 'he can't handle so many trains at once!'

The express was almost at the end of the long straight. It slowed for the curve right, at the bottom. For a brief time after that it would be running directly under the control panel at which Brian was sitting. That would be his chance to make an impression. He hauled himself astride the top log and waited.

The express took the curve at a reduced pace, but squealing slightly nevertheless. Coley could sense most of the load concentrate on the inner wheels. Then he could see his son above him.

He waved frantically.

Brian seemed to rise slightly from his chair. His shadow leapt gigantically ahead of him, stretching forward and up on the slanting ceiling. Behind his head the glare of the Anglepoise lamp was almost unbearable. Coley was unable to make out the features of his son at all: there was only the silhouette. He couldn't tell if he had noticed anything.

With almost despairing violence he flung the lamp. He saw it speed in a low parabola out over the road which ran parallel to the track, bounce on the white space of Brian's shin exposed above his sock, and vanish in the darkness beyond. The enormous figure rose farther, towering now above the speeding express. Coley was sure now that he had been seen. He made desperate motions with his hands, indicating that he would like a total shut-down of power. The boy waved. Coley turned sick. He stared down at his hands, pathetic little signals of distress. The probability was that the boy couldn't even see them.

But he should have been aware that something was wrong. Surely he must see that.

They tore through another station. They were taking the curves now at speed. They flashed across the scores of intersecting rails of the marshalling yard. The noise was like machine-gun fire. He saw another unit come into play: a two-car diesel slipped away south in a coquettish twinkle of chromium.

'He's showing off,' thought Coley grimly, 'he's going to try to bring every bloody train we've got into motion.'

He knew now that the only way he could save himself would be somehow to get off the train. If only he didn't feel so hellishly bushed!

Coley was never tired. Other people seemed to be tired for him. In every project which he had ever undertaken his adherents had flaked away at some stage, forgotten, like the jettisoned elements in a rocket flight. Hector Coley himself drove on to arrive at his object in perfect condition. But now he was tired, and he felt himself nearing exhaustion with his loss of blood and the battering he had taken.

There was just a chance, he thought, of a stop at Coleyville. The boy had evidently taken in the importance of that one. He'd postpone the final effort to get clear until Coleyville was reached.

He leant over the cold metal of which the log was made, and embraced it like a lover. The metal was cold and refreshing against the skin of face and chest. Through his blurring vision he saw again the great grey plain, and the approaching scissors intersection before Coleyville. Once again the smart little roadster ground to a peremptory halt at the crossing. Other cars halted behind it.

But the express did not this time slacken speed. It went through Coleyville at sixty. For a fleeting instant he saw again the maroon face of the guard, the giant blonde, the malevolence of the middle-aged schoolboy. Those waiting waited still. Those who had been waving waved on. Then Coleyville was gone, and the man on the log recognized that he would have to jump for it. He thought ahead.

Wistfully his mind passed over the swimming pool of the country club. If only that had been water! He winced at the appalling idea of crashing through glass.

But where else could he make it? Spring on to the roof of the tunnel, as they entered? But no, the mountain above was too sheer: it would be like flinging himself against a brick wall. Then he remembered the trees which overhung the long straight beyond. He'd been in the Pullman last time they'd gone under those. But he might be able to grab one and hang from it long enough to let the express pass beneath him.

He fainted away.

When he came to he found that the express was emerging from the tunnel. He wondered how many times he had made the circuit. Several times probably. Looking across the countryside from this high vantage point he could see on almost every track trains and cars travelling, east, west, south, north.

He felt a cold wind blowing now powerfully across the track. It was horrendous, roaring. It threatened to drag his very hair out by the roots. The shirt sleeves were flapping like mad, trapped seagulls. He twisted his head to face the blast and looked on at the final horror.

His son had quitted the control panel. He was now squatting, setting a fan on the long grey meadow of carpet. In the whirlwind everything light in the landscape was going over, the waving figures of the yokels and children, the flimsier structures of paper cottages. The station at Coleyville was collapsing, while the people on the platform waited patiently.

Brian smiled. Coley saw him smile.

Then, as he thought that he must be obliged to relinquish his hold and be blown away to destruction, the boy picked the fan up again, and placed it where it always was.

But he did not return to his seat at the control panel. He went out through the door, and shut it behind him. The noise as it slammed was like a shell exploding.

The express went down the long straight through the suspension bridge and towards the curve at the bottom and reached a hundred miles an hour. Coley watched the overhanging branches of the trees sweep towards him. He climbed on to the logs and steadied himself with his feet braced against a knot to make this last leap. He realized that he would have to make it good the first time, and hoist himself well clear of the onrushing roofs of following coaches.

Red, yellow, brown, green, the trees suddenly showed.

He made his effort.

He felt the spines run through his hands. Then the branch broke, and he was jammed in the doorway of the next carriage.

He pulled a spine which had remained in his flesh clear, then lay there. He was broken. He waited for the express to derail.

But it did not derail. It swooped on the curve and screamed round it. Almost exuberantly it hurled itself at the next stretch running below the now abandoned control panel. Behind him he heard but did not see the last light trucks and petrol waggons go somersaulting off the track. For a moment there was a grinding check on the express: the wheels raced, then a link must have snapped and the wheels bit again. They surged forward.

The clatter as they started across the marshalling yard began again.

Coley got up quickly. The will which had devastated board rooms, concentrated now in his tiny figure, was the only part of him which had not been reduced to a scale of one in three hundred. He remembered that before getting on to the express at the outset of this misconceived adventure he had sunk almost to his knees in the foam rubber ballast on which the track was laid. In the marshalling yard there was acres of it! He stepped back on the log-bearing truck and looked quickly about him.

'Foam-rubber,' he said to himself, 'not ballast.'

He flung himself out, as if into a feather bed.

He lay for a moment luxuriously. He watched the express disappear in the direction of shattered Coleyville. He sighed. What a close thing!

Downstairs, Brian was buckling on his raincoat. His mother watched him anxiously.

'I think your father would prefer it if just this once more you helped him with his trains. It's a bit late to go out.'

'No, he sent me away.'

His mother sighed. She looked forward to an uncomfortable scene with Hector when he should deign to reappear. He probably wouldn't even eat his dinner and then be even more bad tempered because he was hungry.

'Don't be out long, then.'

'I'm only going out to Billy's. We're going to watch for a hedgehog he says comes out at night in his garden.'

'All right then, but be sure to wrap up well.'

Coley hauled himself to his feet. He stood alone, a figure of flesh and blood in a world of fakes.

'I shall never play with them again, not after this,' he said quietly.

It was a decision, but it was accurate also as a prophecy. A sibilant hiss was all he heard of the diesel before it struck him. It was travelling at only three miles an hour, or call it sixty.

It killed him.

Before he died, he thought, 'How wretched to die here like this, tiny, probably not even found! They'll wonder whatever became of me.'

He wished he might have been out altogether of the tiny world which had proved to be too big for him. It was his dying wish.

No one doubted that it had been murder when Hector Coley was found stretched out across the toy world which had been his great hobby and pride. But so battered and bloodied and broken a figure could only have resulted from the attack of a maniac of prodigious, overwhelming strength.

'He was still playing with the models when he was surprised,' reported the Inspector, 'the current was on, and about ten of them had come to rest against his body. To be frank, though, he looked as if about ten real ones had hit him.'

manner of thoughts come into being. I said to my wife ...'

The head jerked round. It was as though a button had been pushed, a string pulled, or the last word had triggered some hidden mechanism into sudden action. It was then that the eleven-forty from Benfleet roared past on the up-line, pushing a wedge of air against the train with a heavy crunch. The frantic diddly-da – diddly-da of two trains travelling in opposite directions mixed their thundering rhythms and a wall of sound crashed in around him, as black terror came shrieking across the lighted carriage.

Jeffrey was looking at a dead-white face in which the eyes were gleaming pools of fire-tinted madness, and the skin was stretched tightly over a framework of bones, the black lips parted in a ferocious grin. Even in the midst of his brain-freezing terror, he realized that once it had been a beautiful face; in fact if the eyes were to lose that flame of madness, the mouth that awful grin, youth and beauty would not be all that far away. Her appearance of advanced age was the result of experience – not the passing of years.

Minutes sped by as he gazed upon that face of horror, looking into the blazing eyes, and felt the clammy coldness grow more intense. Then the clenched teeth parted and a harsh whisper came rasping across the carriage.

'He ... lost ... his ... head ...'

The roaring clatter of the passing train suddenly ceased, the overhead lights flickered and went out – and Jeffrey Layne threw back his head, opened his mouth – and screamed.

He came back to consciousness in an empty, lighted carriage, and sat perfectly still for an entire minute, while he tried to remember, to consider – to understand.

Memory returned on reluctant feet, and with it came a mental picture of a dead-white face, with mad-bright eyes and bared teeth. Understanding arrived a little later.

He had seen a ghost.

There was absolutely no manner of doubt in his mind. A ghost – an apparition – a time-image – call it what you like – he had seen it, felt the clammy coldness that was as much part of its make-up as the black cloak, the bonnet, the tasselled scarf; and – heaven preserve him – heard it.

Reaction began to take its toll. He began to shake violently; sweat ran down his face and there came to him the certain knowledge that he was terribly – horrifyingly – alone. Shut up in a small metal box that was hurtling through the night at sixty-odd miles an hour. He glanced up at the communication cord, and once even reached up a trembling hand towards it. Then he slowly withdrew it and huddled back in his corner of the carriage as he accepted the bitter truth. The seer-of-ghosts is never believed, particularly by a guard of a suddenly halted train.

But he would get off at the next station, wheresoever it might be, and trust to luck that he would catch a late bus, or hire a taxi for the remainder of the journey.

Chalkwell Station was shrouded in darkness.

Jeffrey Layne staggered along the deserted platform, dimly aware that his legs felt like sagging rubber, and that now he was out in the open air, a nasty red mist was obscuring his vision and threatening to bring him to his knees at any moment. He came to the tiny square of light that pinpointed the ticket-collector's box, and it was here that the returning weakness had its way with him, for he suddenly swayed, then sank down in the little open gateway.

A tall man with rimless glasses and a slim, pencil-line moustache looked down at him, with an almost comical expression of grave concern. His deep voice was friendly, sympathetic, but above all, human – alive.

'Gracious, sir – let me help you up. Are you ill or ...' He did not finish the sentence, but Jeffrey knew the missing word had been 'drunk'. Assisted by the man's outstretched hand, he clambered to his feet and leaned against the ticket-box.

'No ... I've had a rather nasty shock – ' this was surely the understatement of all time – 'but if I could rest somewhere for a few minutes, I'll be all right.'

'Of course, sir, let me help you into the office. There won't be another train for half an hour and I always make meself a cup of tea about this time.'

Jeffrey was assisted into a small, green-painted room, equipped with an oil-stove, two battered-looking armchairs and a solid, deal table. The ticket-collector dropped two teabags into a brown teapot, then eyed a singing kettle which sat on the oil-stove.

'This nasty shock – something personal was it, sir? Bad news, maybe?'

'No.' Jeffrey wiped his moist forehead and succumbed to the overwhelming urge to tell his story. The fellow would probably think he was mad. 'As a matter of fact – I don't expect you to believe this – I saw a ghost on the train.'

The ticket-collector poured boiling water into the teapot, replaced the kettle on the stove, then nodded gravely.

'That would have been the Woman in Black, no doubt.'

Jeffrey stared up at the man with sagging mouth and bulging eyes. 'You know about her ...?'

The ticket-collector poured tea into two china mugs, then added milk from a half-full bottle. 'Sugar, sir?'

Jeffrey nodded. 'Yes. Two spoonfuls.'

'You've a sweet tooth, sir. Same here. Now, you drink that down, and you'll soon feel yourself again. Nothing like sweet tea when you've suffered a bit of a shock.'

'You know about her?' Jeffrey repeated.

The ticket-collector nodded very slowly as though admitting to a deplorable weakness. 'That I do. I've heard about her for more years than I care to remember, although I've never seen her myself. But a lot of people have and they can't all be liars or madmen. It's rather sad, really.'

'Sad!' Jeffrey exclaimed.

'Yes, sir. Sad. Imagine – the pretty child, who grows up to be a beautiful woman – who becomes a ghost on a train out of Fenchurch Street. Don't you think that's sad?'

Jeffrey nodded and took a deep swig from the mug. Then he asked the obvious question: 'I suppose there is a story?'

The ticket-collector chuckled. 'Bless your heart, sir, of course there is. Can't have a ghost without a story, can you now?' He paused and looked reflectively at the little red window on the oil-stove. 'Her name was Clara Bowman.'

Jeffrey was feeling much better. The train was now miles away, the experience seemed to have happened in a different time dimension. Now he was inclined to be jocular.

'Suits her,' he said.

'You're right there, sir,' the ticket-collector agreed. 'A fine upstanding wench. Came from a good family, met up with a young fellow from down Benfleet way. Got herself in trouble, if you follow my meaning – a terrible thing back in those days. Particularly as he was by no means acceptable to her family. They ran off together, meaning to get married in Southend, and spend their honeymoon at Thorpe Bay. Ever been there, sir?'

Jeffrey said he hadn't and waited impatiently for the rest of the story.

'Lovely place – particularly in spring. Any road, on the way down from London, the young fellow decides to look out of the window. Just then a train comes round a bend, intended husband has his head sticking out like a balloon on the end of a stick – and bash – the train knocks it off.'

Jeffrey said: 'Good God!'

'Your feelings do you credit, sir. The headless body falls back on to the lap of the prospective bride and in no time at all she's soaked in blood. When the train drew into Southend they found her cradling the headless body in her arms and singing a lullaby to it.'

'Mad, of course,' Jeffrey suggested.

'As a hatter, sir. She had her baby in a looney bin – if you will pardon the expression. But that's not the end of the story.'

Jeffrey looked meaningly at the teapot and the ticket-collector obligingly refilled his mug.

'There's more?'

'Has to be, doesn't there, sir? Otherwise, she wouldn't be haunting the 23.05 from Fenchurch Street. These things run to a pattern. Maybe somebody was careless, or maybe she was very cunning. They say mad people are. Anyway, she caught the same train, and at the very spot where her poor young man had his head knocked off, a few seconds before the up train came round the bend, she opens the door and throws herself out. I bet it upset the other passengers no end.'

'That I can believe,' Jeffrey observed with deep sincerity.

They did not speak again for some time and Jeffrey was wondering if he could find the courage to climb aboard the next train, when the ticket-collector murmured:

'I expects you're curious as to how I know that story so pat, sir?'

Jeffrey shrugged. 'I assumed you had been told.'

The man chuckled. It was a deep, rich, almost sinister sound. 'You're right there. You haven't forgotten the baby, have you, sir? The one she had in the asylum? It grew up and became my old dad, sir.'

Jeffrey's flagging interest was now fully revived.

'Good God, man, that means ...'

The ticket-collector smiled gently. 'That's right, sir. The Woman in Black is my grannie. Interesting, ain't it?'

Jeffrey looked up at the tall thin figure and for the first time noted the pale skin, stretched so tightly over the framework of bones, saw the bright glitter in his eyes, observed the white teeth bared in a near-ferocious grin. A long, lean hand, that had more than a passing resemblance to a claw, reached out and grasped his arm. The deep voice was wistful.

'She must come through this old station every night, sir. But never once has she got off to see me. I mean to say ... I am her own flesh and blood. Showing herself to strangers ... Gracious me, are you off, sir?'

For a man who had suffered a recent terrible experience, Jeffrey made very good time down the platform and out through the ticket-barrier.

He now travels to town by Green Line bus.

XII

Synopsis of a Nightmare
Peter C. Smith

The greater part of the terror and horror of dying is the dread of being on one's own.

Perhaps if one were trapped with a ghastly and doomladen apparition in a coach full of football fans celebrating a heavy win over a rival team, or on a day outing to Margate, the edge would be taken off the fear.

If there is anything at all cheering to be gleaned from World War III then perhaps it is the thought that, in the words of the song, 'We'll all go together when we go'. But mayhap the fear of death is so great that, if possible, we would like to check first for some reassurance ...

Roger Blair pushed aside the dog-eared typescript with a sigh and leaned back in his chair. He shut his eyes briefly, put his hands behind his head and lay for a moment relaxed. The July sunlight beat in through the panes of his office window on to his uplifted face and for twopence he could have slept.

'God, this won't do', he said aloud to himself and dropped the chair forward again, opening his eyes and surveying his cluttered desk top with a sigh of irritation. He rummaged among the letters and dust jackets until he found his cigarettes, drew one from a half-empty packet and then began searching for the matches. The heat in the room was ghastly.

Outside, the muffled beat of the endless traffic murmured and roared against his ears like the beating of the surf on a beach. His window was slightly open at the top, it being of the old sash-type, and the reek of petrol fumes wafted in from the Strand and mingled with the stale air of his room. His head ached abominably. He found the matches under a box folder, lit his cigarette and looked at his watch. 'Four-thirty already, damn and blast', he groaned.

He strove to think. The manuscript he had just read through was ghastly, no other word for it, but how was he to tell Sir Milne Murray that, without upsetting the old buffer? Come to think of it, how was he to do it without upsetting Sir Richard himself. He glared at the ceiling trying to penetrate the floor of his employer's office above. He knew the two men were friends from way back, which was probably the only reason that the blasted typescript had landed on his desk anyway. Sir Richard, he knew, would expect constructive criticism, but, better, a damn good reason for rejecting the memoirs of a crony. Why him?

July already and next year's Spring books still not finalised ... He stubbed out his cigarette angrily and reached for his schedule. Hmmmm. Not *too* bad. Six titles sent off to the printers, jackets in hand, eight. A hell of a lot of editing on two others, might have to put them back to the following autumn. Tight, but possible. Trouble was their old stalwart, Davidson, was running out of form. 'Which reminds me!' he said aloud again, 'where is Davidson?'

Stuart Davidson was one of Symond & Steele's 'regular' authors. That is to say, he wrote a book a year for them, each of which had a steady sale of around two thousand copies, good, bad or indifferent, and thus, as Symond & Steele were geared to survival, and a very satisfactory living, on producing forty such books a year which did just that, Davidson was a rock against the uncertainties of mishmash like Sir Milne Murray and his ilk.

But for the first time in eleven steady, reliable years Davidson had not turned in his copy on the contract date. It would have to be *this* bloody year of all years, with nothing else to shove in its place. Damn the man. Anyway, perhaps he would yet do the right thing. He was supposed to have an appointment at 4.30 to explain the reason for the delay. With any luck he'd have worked all weekend and finished it after all. 'Please', prayed Blair, 'please let it be so.'

He looked at his watch again. Four-forty.

He got up, and, lighting another cigarette, walked over to the window. Below him, Southampton Street, leading from the

Strand to Old Covent Garden, was jammed solid with traffic. Taxi drivers were fuming, a straying tourist coach was stuck behind a parked lorry and a disinterested traffic warden was adjusting her cap in the window of Thomas Cook's. Half in the street from the Strand he spotted a purple Toyota with the window wound down and an anxious bespectacled face thrust out, and he knew why Davidson was late.

Eventually the traffic sorted itself out, as it always seems to in London, and Davidson's car inched up to the kerb outside the office, mounted it and stalled. The driver got out hastily into the path of a messenger scooter, received some verbal abuse, to which he seemed immune, and disappeared inside, away from Blair's view. As he watched, the meter maid finished adjusting her stocking seams and, seeing the jam was free, resumed her duty. Blair noted wryly how she soon spotted the Toyota and made a purposeful advance upon it, undoing her satchel and reaching for her pencil with obvious relish.

'Tough luck, my old son', murmured Blair, 'You'll have to put it on expenses.'

A few minutes later his intercom buzzed.

'Yes Tracey', he said, 'I've seen the old boy. Bung him in, luv.'

'Mr Davidson is here, Mr Blair'. He smiled as Tracey went through the routine for the benefit of the visitor. 'Ask him to go in? Of course. Mr Blair is expecting you, sir.'

'You are beautiful', he whispered into the intercom, and switched off before she could reply. There was a knock at his office door.

Davidson edged his way in nervously. Blair, forgetting his production problems for the moment, and thinking of 'Rita, Rita the Meter Maid' busy adorning his guest's windscreen outside, repressed a grin and turned it into a welcoming smile.

'Hello, Stuart. Nice to see you.'

They shook hands. Davidson's palm was hot and sticky. Ugh!

Blair removed several box files from the only other chair in his tiny room, for which Davidson was grateful, and kept murmuring his thanks, and his apologies at being so late.

'It's only a quarter of an hour or so,' replied Roger to put him at ease. 'Cigarette?'

He knew Davidson was a non-smoker, but to his surprise the author accepted with alacrity and took one in a shaking hand. Blair lit it for him, rescued the ashtray from the window seat and sat down.

'Look here. I'm awfully sorry about all this', said Davidson. He was too, it was obvious. He was apologetic, crestfallen and a bag of nerves. Blair felt sorry for him.

'Well it's not that bad, Stuart', he replied. 'You are two months late, but we can make it up, I feel sure. You have never needed much editing on your work.' He smiled. 'Have you brought it in?'

'Well actually, no,' muttered Davidson, crimsoning up. 'I just cannot finish it. I'm sorry.' Sweat stood out on his brow. He stubbed the half-smoked cigarette out and looked blindly out of the window. His fingers knotted themselves together and his leg shook.

Blair cursed inwardly, but only concern showed on his face. The man was a nervous wreck, what the hell was wrong. After a while he prised the story out of the man.

'It's nightmares', said Davidson, looking at the carpet, 'don't laugh. Actually,' he went on, eager now to confide in someone, 'It's the *same* nightmare. Night after night. For months now. It won't stop. Won't go away.'

'Lots of people have nightmares, Stuart', said Blair. 'It's nothing to be ashamed of. Have you seen a doctor?' He buzzed the intercom. 'Send in some coffee, will you, Tracey,' he asked. He lit another cigarette and handed it to Davidson.

'Doctor. Yes, of course,' replied the author shortly. 'All the usual things, nothing works. And the dream. It's so real, so clear. Crystal clear. And it never changes. Every night, exactly the same nightmare.'

There was a welcome break while Tracey slid in with the coffee which Davidson, as with everything else, accepted with pathetic gratitude. Blair watched Tracey's hips in her summer dress as she swayed out, sighed, then brought his mind back to his problem author.

'Would it help to tell me about the nightmare?' he asked.

Davidson sipped his coffee. 'Yes, it can't hurt. I've told others. Nobody can explain it and nobody can make it go away. But you might as well hear it.'

And, after a pause, he began.

'I am in a car, travelling at a normal speed, not hurrying, through flat, unhedged, countryside, with long views of nothing but crop-laden land and openness. The road is dead-straight and unending, without curve or hedgerow or fence, but I am somehow aware of a wood extending from the right-hand side almost to the side of the road in a thin wedge. Towering over this woodland finger, just behind it as my car approaches, is a great aqueduct. Huge arches, curving high above me, carry a ruined waterway. The aqueduct crosses the road and ends abruptly. It has crumbled away but there are no signs of fallen masonry at the base of its termination.

'I become aware of another towering structure, miles away, but quite distinct. Even higher than the aqueduct, it is huge. A motorway on colossal piles is under construction. As I become aware of this I can hear a truck full of building materials roaring along it, high above us and far off.

'The motorway also ends abruptly, like the aqueduct, and again, although I know it is under construction, there is no sign of life, save the sound of this truck, which I *know* is full of building materials, rushing along it at high speed towards its end. Although the sun is hot, it has been raining just before.

'I turn to a companion beside me in the car I am driving and say: "My God, I wouldn't want his job. With the roadway up there wet and at that speed he will have to brake soon or he'll go over the edge." My companion laughs and replies: "They know what they are doing."

'As he mocks my fears the truck does indeed screech to a skidding halt, goes out of control, and then plunges off the end of the motorway into the sky. As it does so our own car passes under the ancient aqueduct and beneath one of the last arches on the left-hand side of the road. It is then that I notice for the first time a large black car, parked, with a family inside. They are admiring the view, in the shade, out of the hot sun. I think it funny not to have noticed it before and I think: "If they are not careful that old ruin will fall on top of them."

'We pass under the arch, my car is going faster in my urge to be under and clear of it. Again my companion laughs, I am horrified, as he has seen the fate of the lorry. Then, again as I predicted, just as we are clear, huge blocks of masonry *do* fall down as the earth shakes. Debris surrounds the parked car, I can see it in my rear-view mirror, the people inside are screaming. My companion shouts for me to stop and go back to help them. But although I slow down I don't stop.

'Then suddenly the aqueduct *explodes* and huge blocks of stone pulverise the trapped car and its screaming occupants. At the same instant I look over to the elevated motorway and see that it too is collapsing and falling in upon itself. As I look over to the left, watching it suddenly disintegrating, I see, streaking towards us as we accelerate, from the far distant horizon, a wall of flame along the ground. As it rushes towards us I can see that it is a huge rift in the earth's crust opening up, with flames shooting up from it as it goes. It is clear that the great crack, which is rushing and flaming at us, will cross the road, and I push hard on the pedal with all my might to outrun it.

'I think to myself: The Bomb. They have dropped the Bomb and a chain reaction is spreading across the country. We are going to outrun it and then, supreme horror, I see another rift streaking towards us from the left, parallel to the first, but on a course I know will pass ahead of us.

'There is no escape. The twin infernoes are almost on us, and the world vanishes in a screaming, searing, scorching chaos of cries and destruction ...'

Davidson was sweating at the end of this recital. He looked up, staring, to see what Blair had made of it. He trembled. Blair was also shaken inside at the intensity of the feeling contained in the man's narration. For once he was lost for words immediately.

Finally they came; futile, empty words of course, but all he could muster.

'Look here, old man,' he quietly soothed. 'You shouldn't be here. What you need is a long rest, not driving across London with your nerves shot like this. What I'm going to recommend is that we postpone the book until next summer, how does that suit you? Take a nice long rest from writing and just relax.' He went on for a while in a similar vein, but the hopeless look in Davidson's eyes told him that his attempts to smooth over the fears were obvious, and, after a further brief exchange, Davidson left.

Blair watched him drive away with the parking ticket still on his window. It brought some sort of normality and humour back but the effects of the tale were still strong. 'I hope you make it', he thought to himself. If ever a man was on the edge of a major crack-up that man was Davidson. He had a long drive ahead of him too, living as he did, out in the wilds beyond Newmarket.

After a while Blair turned back to his work but Davidson's strange tale kept intruding on his mind. The afternoon wore on and it got hotter.

He was re-reading the Murray manuscript when the intercom buzzed.

'Yes Tracey', he said.

'It's a call for you on line one', she replied. 'Davidson's wife, about why he can't come in after all.'

'But he's already been in, what is she talking about?' he replied testily.

'I don't understand you, Mr Blair,' answered the girl. 'He *was* due in, at 4.30, but he hasn't arrived yet. Will you speak to his wife now?'

'Put in the call', he snapped angrily, and she did so.

Mrs Davidson was in tears. He supressed his anger and incomprehension to hear her out. There was a lot of interference on the line and some chaos the other end but he made out that Davidson had just been killed in some massive accident. A car crash or something, just fifteen minutes ago. She was near hysterical and then the line went completely dead. Blair's head was reeling. She said something about a huge pile-up, or something, on the main road to London, near the new M.11 spur.

He sat and looked at his watch. It was four-forty. He got up and looked out of his window. Below him, Southampton Street was jammed solid with traffic. Taxi drivers were fuming, a straying tourist coach was stuck behind a parked lorry and a disinterested traffic warden was adjusting her cap in the window of Thomas Cook's.

Blair felt sick. He sat down quickly. His mind raced. Obviously he had fallen asleep but his dream was identical to what was now happening. He called for Tracey, and when she came in, her pretty face taut and angry, he apologised. She sat on the side of his desk with concern and he related what had happened. She was sensible as well as pretty. She didn't laugh at him.

'It's remarkable,' she said eventually, 'but I've heard of similar cases, haven't you?'

'Do you believe in ghosts then, Tracey,' he asked her wearily but with a faint smile.

'I might do if it had happened to me,' she replied openly.

'Well *my* ghost seemed certain we were all to die, all doomed, not just himself.'

He frowned as he remembered Davidson's fantastic story. 'Perhaps it's just me who is cracking up.'

'But don't you *see*', replied Tracey. 'When you die it's the *same* thing. Everyone else *is* dead, to *you*, to all intents and purposes. Gone. Wiped out. His ghost could no more accept that he was to go out alone than his living self would have wanted to. It was too close to the event. His spirit had not had time to accept the verdict of fate.'

'Yes, that must be the logical, if that's the word, answer', he mused. 'It must be ...'

Outside the office window the sky turned white. The shock-wave from the second bomb reached central London within seconds, that of the first, which had landed slightly off-course in Cambridge, being muffled by the hills to the north of the capital fifteen minutes earlier ...

XIII

Non-Paying Passengers
R. Chetwynd-Hayes

R. Chetwynd-Hayes has for many years delighted followers of the supernatural with his sophisticated short stories of which he has published several collections. He is also now the editor of the Fontana series of Ghost Stories. As well as being a fine writer, and a fine editor, he also has a nice sense of atmosphere; here he recreates the claustrophobic one of the District Line at rush-hour.

Walk down any busy street. Sit in a crowded restaurant. Take a seat in a well-filled cinema. In particular, board a packed train. The chances are that somewhere in the immediate vicinity is a ghost. An actual, visible, audible, and – heaven help us – a solid ghost.

This is an unpalatable truth, that would be greeted with derision were it widely broadcast. Certainly, Percy Fortesque would have become gravely embarrassed if such a possibility had been presented to him as an undeniable fact, his assumption being he was either in the presence of a crank or a madman.

He was therefore totally unprepared when he saw the face of his dead wife staring at him from a window of the five-forty-five train which was standing at Platform 16 at Waterloo Station. She was sitting in the corner seat, wearing that blank, long-suffering look he remembered so well, and her steel-rimmed glasses reflected the light from an overhead platform lamp, so that they resembled miniature suns.

Percy's heart gave one violent thump and the shock froze his reasoning powers into icy splinters of fear, so that he could only keep walking and finally seat himself in the compartment next to the driver's cab. Then his brain gradually resumed its natural function and thoughts came tripping over one another in a vain effort to present a rational theory.

'That woman could not possibly have been Doris.' He repeated this comforting assertion over and over again, and was delighted to note a marked improvement in his morale. He then moved on to list a number of excellent reasons why a defunct wife could not possibly be travelling on the five-forty-five from Waterloo. 'One, she's dead. I was with her when she died. She said: "Oh, dear," and died. Two, she was cremated and her ashes sprinkled under a rosebush.' Percy was very pleased now that he had decided on cremation. The fire was so final. Old-fashioned burial meant the component parts were still around. The bones still in existence. The skull intact. And ... goodness gracious ... sealed up in a wooden box, she could still be in one piece. But the cremation oven disintegrated; it was as though she had never been. She did not exist.

Then his nasty, inquiring brain recalled the memory of that face framed in a train window and began to go over the salient points. She had been wearing that awful blue hat that Percy had so detested; and ... oh, good Lord ... there had been that little wen on the left side of her chin. The comforting thought of a Doris double began to fade. Surely the arm of coincidence could not be that long? But what was the alternative? Percy shifted uneasily and a dour-faced woman to his left shot him a suspicious glance. A Doris-ghost on a rush-hour train? An apparition on the five-forty-five? Percy giggled and the dour-faced woman tried to edge away.

When he alighted at Richmond he had to have a second look. His heart once again began to beat unnaturally fast and anticipation made icy fingers to trail down his spine – but he had to seek reassurance. Surely a second look would prove beyond doubt that he had been mistaken. Been deceived by a trick of light. Deluded by a quirk of imagination.

He walked slowly along the platform, daring to look into each window, and disinterested faces stared back at him. Newspapers were rustled, one saucy-eyed girl winked at him, but so far there was no sign of *the* face. A whistle blew, a voice shouted: 'Right, Charlie!' and the train began to draw away. Percy stopped and faced the train as the carriages flashed by.

Then, just as hope was maturing into blessed relief, he had a glimpse of Doris's face. Blue hat, steel-rimmed glasses, wen and all. He had the impression that just as the carriage tore out of his line of view, she turned her head so as to get a last look at him.

It really was too much. He fainted on the platform and a porter revived him with a cup of tea from the station buffet.

Percy had a good worry all night, and so rose completely unrefreshed next morning. The shaving mirror reflected lines around his mouth and his eyes looked like red-rimmed saucers with blue centres. But nevertheless, the short passage of time had worn the horror down to a nagging uncertainty. Perhaps there was a woman who exactly resembled Doris, right down to an unfortunate taste in hats and a facial disfigurement. It was unlikely, but not impossible. Percy spoke aloud, a not unusual occurrence since he had been living alone.

'I should have got into the carriage and sat beside her.'

Next time he would, even if there was only standing room, and face this woman, eye to eye. In fact he would open some kind of conversation with her. How about: 'Forgive me, but you have an amazing resemblance to my late wife. I hope you don't mind my mentioning it.' She would have to make some kind of response, even if it was only to tell him to push off, and then the bubble would burst. The illusion would shatter. She could not possibly have Doris's voice. Not that low, precise whisper. He hoped she would have a voice like a fog-horn. That would settle the matter once and for all.

Three weeks passed without so much as a glimpse of anyone who remotely looked like Doris and uncertainty disintegrated into doubt. 'Maybe ...' dissolved and became, 'Impossible!' The gasp of fear went out as an echo which returned as a laugh of self-ridicule. Peace of mind gave one last look back along the darkened avenues of time, then, like a well-fed cat, settled down before the fire of complacency and purred its contentment. Percy ceased to examine crowded railway carriages.

The expected never happens. The unexpected pounces on the unprepared from the commonplace. Before Percy boarded the District train he had to travel on the Underground, and it was here that his peace of mind was shattered for ever. He was seated in a compartment that was full but not crowded. Every seat was taken, but a few people were standing by the doors, where they either strap-hung or slouched, while wearing that look of painful resignation which is peculiar to their kind. Percy Fortesque was solving the *Evening Standard* crossword puzzle and only looked up when the train roared into Charing Cross station. His eyes photographed the curved walls, the passengers seated opposite, and the extreme side view of the strap-hangers and slouchers by the door. The brain automatically developed the pictures so meticulously captured by the eyes and began to store them away in the dark recess which is the lumber-room of memory. Then it grabbed one back and retained it for the soul's consideration. At first the soul did not want to know. It swiftly thrust the picture into the lumber-room and slammed the door. The brain suggested a retake. The soul vetoed the idea. The brain, being the irritating, curiosity-ridden organ that it was, insisted. Percy, with great reluctance, lowered his newspaper and looked towards the door. There was no manner of doubt. Doris was hanging on to a strap and staring at him.

Absolutely no shred of comforting, sanity-saving doubt. Blue hat, steel-rimmed glasses, wen, shabby grey coat, slightly wrinkled stockings and sensible shoes. Nothing missing. She had that blank, long-suffering expression, which suggested she was expecting him to do something, but knew very well that he wouldn't. Outside on the platform a voice commanded: 'Mind the doors,' and the doors obediently slid together. Then the voice made a noise that sounded like 'Ye ... up,' and the train jerked into motion. But Percy continued to stare back at his late wife. This should have been an excellent opportunity for him to try out his theory and stand beside her, but he was too petrified to move, let alone talk.

The train took its time in getting to Waterloo. Just as though wishing to prolong the agony, it stopped twice, and once, to Percy's great horror, the lights flickered as if considering the possibility of going out. It was then that Doris broke the spell. She jerked her head round and stared at an advertisement for Gordon's Gin, and freedom of movement returned. Fear withdrew a little way, and Percy was able to clear his mind of panic-debris.

Suppose – just suppose that someone with a warped, perverted sense of humour were playing a distasteful, but, oh, Lord, soul-saving practical joke. Suppose they had found Doris's double and dressed her up in a replica of Doris's clothes – that would be a rational explanation. But it was not a very convincing one. Belatedly he began to consider his original intention of getting up and speaking to her, but scarcely had he flexed his leg muscles than the train rushed into Waterloo Underground station and a crowd of passengers had risen from their seats. The doors sighed, then slid open and Doris was swept out on to the platform, and Percy, a few yards behind, saw her blue hat bobbing up and down like a rogue buoy in a rough sea.

He kept her in sight when the crowd surged into a side passage and had forced his way within three bodies' distance when the queue formed for the lift. It was then that he noticed how still she was. There was not even the slightest suggestion of movement. No shifting of feet, no jerk of the head, no wriggling of shoulders, no – now he came to think of it – rise and fall that denotes breathing. One might suppose that here was an automaton with its engine switched off.

A roaring of displaced air announced the arrival of the lift; the door crashed open and a ticket collector stood to one side with outstretched hand. He snatched at tickets with all the enthusiasm of a fruit-picker gathering strawberries, but when Doris passed him he gave her a single glance, then instantly turned his attention to the next passenger. Percy was positive that he had seen her, but it was as though his brain had rejected her presence. It was this simple action that finally convinced Percy he was in fact following the ghost of his dead wife. There was something terribly familiar about the man's swift glance, followed by that air of total rejection. He, Percy, must have done it many times. Possibly everyone had at one time or another. You saw and instantly forgot what you had seen. But, once in a million times, someone forgot to forget. Then they were haunted.

The lift gave a great sigh and stopped. The crowd surged

out and Percy followed Doris, first up a short flight of steps, then up a slight incline and out into the main station. The blue hat bobbed its way towards Platform 16, and again a ticket collector gave her one swift glance before scowling at a little man who had forgotten to show his season ticket.

Doris walked slowly along the platform until she found a carriage with the door open. She climbed in and sank down into a corner seat and looked dejectedly out of the window. Percy, after vainly trying to curb the brain's damnable lust for knowledge, performed the most courageous act of his life. He bounded into the carriage and sat down beside her.

He was ignored. The still figure was a study in non-movement. Percy's trembling hands opened a newspaper and spread it out, before he dared look sideways. Again he had a close-up view of a scrawny neck, with thin grey hair combed up into an unbecoming bun, which in some small measure supported the blue hat. What would happen if he were to touch her? Nothing on earth could have made him experiment, but speech was a kind of abstract contact. If those waxen-looking ears still functioned she might hear a whispered inquiry, always supposing that he could force his tongue to make one.

Three times his vocal cords contracted, three times his lips parted, and it was not until he had closed his eyes and taken a very deep breath that he was able to send out one whispered word.

'Doris?'

At that moment the train jerked into violent movement and the figure swayed, so that for an awful, heart-thumping eternity Percy thought it was going to fall back against him. Then the train assumed an even, clack-a-de-clack speed, and the figure once again became a study in still-life. Although Percy could not think this was a good simile. He gathered his courage and breath and expelled the latter in a whispered question.

'Doris – is that you?'

The head came slowly round and the steel-rimmed spectacles gave him one expressionless stare, then the bloodless lips parted and an answering whisper said: 'You're late.'

It was perhaps unfortunate that Percy had not noticed he had boarded the slow train, because, even as he was digesting this piece of disturbing information, it slowed down and stopped at Vauxhall Station. When someone opened the door, Doris, without removing her expressionless stare from his face, climbed down on to the platform with a kind of crab-like movement. She remained stationary while a porter slammed the door, but, as the train pulled away, Percy thought he detected a slight, irritated shaking of the head.

As may be imagined, he was very unhappy and decided to seek expert advice.

Madame Orloff (Medium Extraordinaire – Messages from the Beyond a Speciality) no longer touted for business. Gone were the days when she handed out cards at railway stations and accosted perfect strangers. Now a discreet advertisement in the *Apparition*:

MADAME ORLOFF IS PREPARED TO CONSIDER A FEW RECOMMENDED ADDITIONS TO HER SELECT CLIENTELE

was all that was needed to keep body and soul together in the manner to which both had grown accustomed. She was not, therefore, at all pleased when she answered an urgent ringing of her doorbell and discovered a distraught Percy on the front step. Neither was she prepared to be gracious.

'Yes?'

Percy made a motion which suggested he was wiping his feet, prior to making an uninvited entry.

'You are Madame Orloff? The medium?'

'The famous medium. Yes.'

'Could I ... could I speak to you for a few minutes?'

'About what?'

Percy dry-washed his hands, looked from left to right, inspected his shoes, then re-routed his attention to Madame Orloff's full figure.

'Well ... it's my wife. She's been dead ...'

'Passed over,' Madame corrected.

'Yes, passed over for six months. But I keep seeing her on the District train.'

'A distinct possibility. It makes a break for the poor dears after a stint on the Circle Line. So what?'

'Well ... I'd like to see you about it.'

Madame Orloff withdrew from her doorway with some reluctance.

'Very well. But I can't give you long. I've got a possession coming in half an hour – by appointment. And I usually has a little kip before I does any casting out.'

She led her unexpected and unrecommended client across the hall and ushered him into a room that was situated at the rear of the house. Here Percy was all but pushed into a chair, then the medium seated herself behind an impressive desk.

'Right. Let's get down to it, then. What sort of party was your wife? Strong-minded? Liked to have things just so?'

Percy nodded. 'You could say so. Mind you, she was quiet. Didn't say much. But she had a will of her own.'

Madame Orloff gave him a shrewd glance that took in his neat, well-brushed suit, polished shoes and the way he clutched his hat in both hands.

'And I expect you used to help her? Do a few jobs round the house? Bit of washing-up, maybe?'

Percy's eyes widened with astonishment and his respect for Madame's exceptional psychic powers grew.

'Yes. How did you know?'

The medium shrugged. 'There's not much hid from us that has the gift. Now, how many times have you seen your wife on the train?'

'Twice on the District and once on the Underground.'

Madame Orloff shook her head angrily. 'That Underground! If I had my way I'd have it blown up. What with it being a cess-pit for elementals, demons, poltergeists and hobgoblins, to say nothing of millions of misguided souls like your passed-over, it's a wonder to me anyone has the nerve to go down there. Talk about possession! What! The number of stories I could tell you of people who came up with something they didn't go down with. Any road, at least your missus has a bit of initiative. She changes over to the District now and again.'

Percy frowned. 'But, what I can't understand – what's she doing on the trains?'

Madame Orloff smiled grimly. 'You may well ask. It's

become a sort of habit with 'em. In my young days I doubt if you'd have come across a travelling hunter once in a blue moon. Now – stone the crows – British Railways and London Transport attract 'em like flies to gum paper. I suppose it's because the earth-bounds like to keep moving, and you've got to admit the trains do move sometimes. The rush hours are best, of course. They can get around without giving offence, if you get my meaning.'

Percy tried to absorb all this information, but one question still had to be satisfactorily answered.

'Doris used to go to chapel three times every Sunday and I'm sure she never thought that trains – well, would be the ultimate destination.'

'Ah, she's waiting, ducks, ain't she? Waiting for her little hubby to come and give her a hand. Stands to reason. All of 'em are mostly waiting for someone. Ever spoken to her?'

Percy hesitated for a moment, then he nodded.

'Yes. Once.'

Madame Orloff beamed her approval. 'That's nice. People are sometimes backwards in coming forward when it comes to having a chat with the passed-over. What did she say?'

'She said … I was late.'

Had he looked up at that moment he might have detected a hint of embarrassment in Madame's rather protuberant eyes. She began to trace a pattern on the desk top with a pudgy forefinger.

'I'm sure that was very nice, dear. Tell me, have you been rather poorly lately? Been off your grub?'

Percy assumed the expression of a rabbit who is beginning to understand the purpose of a cooking-pot.

'No. I feel fine. Absolutely fine.'

Madame Orloff raised her thick eyebrows as though to denote surprise. Then she continued to trace an invisible pattern on the desk-top.

'I'm pleased to hear that, dear. Very pleased. But your dear passed-over did say you were late. Didn't she?'

'Yes.' Percy wriggled slightly in his chair. 'I've been trying to understand what she meant.'

'Well, it don't take much gumption to work that out. I mean to say, you don't need a college education. She meant you were late. Overdue. All behind, as the saying goes. Follow me, dear?'

Percy swallowed and turned to an interesting shade of pale green.

'You mean ...?'

'Yes, I do. You should have been doing the old Circle Line for some time. Had any near misses lately? You know, almost fell downstairs or something of that nature?'

'I did almost drown in the municipal swimming baths, but an attendant pulled me out just in time. He said I was lucky, as he should have been off duty.'

Madame Orloff nodded her satisfaction. 'That would be it. You should have gone then. I expect your dear passed-over was put out. Never mind, she'll try to put things right, so I wouldn't worry too much.'

'You mean ... I'm going to have another accident?'

'I'd say you can bet on it. Your good lady sounds like a very determined soul to me and her patience must be wearing a bit thin. Well, it stands to reason. So you go home and leave it all to her. Is there anything wrong?'

There was a good reason for her inquiry because Percy was on his feet and making all haste towards the door. He was also shaking his head in frantic denial and trying to express his total disbelief by shouting: 'I don't believe you. Doris would never do this to me.'

Madame Orloff grinned as she heaved her considerable bulk from the chair. 'Don't kid yourself. She won't half give you gyp when the time comes. No woman likes to be kept waiting.'

Percy was out of the room and running for the front door and was in no condition to heed Madame's cry of rage.

'What about me fee? I don't do this for peanuts.'

The Green Line bus service gained another regular passenger.

Percy derived a kind of grim pleasure imagining Doris looking for him vainly on either the five-forty-five train or in the Underground. It was rather like that time he had dodged chapel and gone to Sunday cinema instead. Then he shuddered as he remembered that Doris had been waiting for him in the foyer. She had an uncanny knack of knowing what he would do next and there was no reason to suppose that a change of location would have dulled her perceptive powers.

For three days and nights he imitated a man sitting on an unexploded bomb. Then on the fourth – a Thursday, which had never been his lucky day – the bus decided to terminate its journey at Hammersmith, and the driver looked round at his passengers with an expression of quiet triumph and ordered: 'All change. 'S'far as we go.'

Percy was faced with a problem. He could either wait for another bus, which would mean arriving at the office half an hour late, or – take to the Underground! There was no reason to suppose that Doris was down there; on the other hand, there was no certainty that she was not. Good heavens, she might be waiting for him on the platform. It was while considering this mind-shattering prospect that Percy happened to look up and see his late wife watching him from the other side of the road.

A stream of cars went by. They were closely followed by two lorries, one hearse and a double-decker bus, then Percy was able to derive the full benefit of Doris's expressionless stare. Suddenly, she raised her arm and beckoned. It was an imperious gesture. The kind of impatient, irritated wave that had on many occasions greeted him from the front gate whenever he arrived home late. He was used to it. It had become an essential part of married life and had created a kind of built-in reflex which meant Percy usually broke into a little trot. It did not fail now. Without further thought he stepped into the road, became aware of the sound of screeching brakes, before a powerful hand pulled him back on to the pavement. Doris made a savage gesture of extreme annoyance before she walked quickly towards the Underground station.

'Tired of life, I dare say,' the burly constable remarked caustically.

'No ... Oh dear, no.'

'Suicide is not illegal,' the constable went on, 'but it's a bit rough on us blokes if we have to scrape you off the road.'

'I'm so sorry. I wouldn't want to be any trouble.'

'Then use your bloody eyes.'

Eventually Percy hired a taxi.

Next morning Doris was on the Green Line bus.

Percy did not see her at first. In fact, it was not until they were passing Barnes Common that he spotted her reflection in the window. She was seated on the opposite side of the aisle, two rows back, and indulging in her usual practice of looking out of the window. Percy trembled and flirted with the idea of getting out at the next stop, only there did not seem to be much point. She would doubtlessly follow him, and the traffic was moving too fast for comfort.

There comes a point when familiarity blunts the sharp edge of fear. It is then that the unusual assumes the appearance of the commonplace and mental disturbance the aspect of a calm sea. Percy, without being aware of the fact, had been becoming gradually accustomed to seeing his late wife on public transport and might have eventually accepted this state of affairs, had he not been aware of her lamentable intentions. As it was, he found himself considering defensive measures, while not forgetting to keep a wary eye on Doris, who, he fancied, was watching his reflection in the window.

The simple solution, if he were not to meet with the destined accident, was to be constantly alert and make absolutely certain there was always a safe distance between them. For an apparition she looked remarkably solid and might quite well be capable of meting out a good shove, should a suitable occasion arise. He must ignore all gestures that demanded haste, look both ways before he crossed the road, hang on to the black moving rail when he went down an escalator, and mind the step when he got out of a Tube train. In fact the list seemed endless, and his heart sank when he considered the task before him. But surely, if he lasted out long enough, she would give up.

When the bus reached Hyde Park Corner, he made a dash for the door, then tore along the pavement clutching his brief-case in one hand and his umbrella in the other. At the entrance to the underpass he looked back. So far as he could see, Doris had not followed him. It was a small victory, but at least she must now realize that her attentions were not welcome.

From then on life was never dull. Percy found there was safety in speed – just so long as he looked where he was going.

When he found Doris waiting at the bus stop he ran for the railway station. When she presented herself at the top of the escalator, he made all haste for the stairs. The merest glimpse of her on the five-forty-five sent him scurrying for the Underground.

But of course all this activity was very wearing, and Percy lost so much weight he wondered if there was any need to worry unduly about a fatal accident. People acquired the habit of giving him pitying looks and even, on occasion, making unfortunate remarks. An ancient aunt, whom he had not seen for some time, gave him one horrified look and said: 'A thin corpse makes an easy burying,' and fear, which up to then had been content to walk in his footsteps, leapt upon his shoulders.

But the body still did not want to die, so the brain was ordered to devise a plan that would keep death forever locked in tomorrow. Such a burden had not been placed upon that idle, curiosity-ridden organ for many a year, but it did its poor best to explore every avenue of escape and finally came up with a proposed solution that brought a glimmer of hope to the darkness of Percy's despair.

Why not, instead of running, walk beside? In fact, better still – follow. Let the hauntee become the haunter. Give her a dose of her own medicine. Percy actually did a little dance of joy round the kitchen when the full beauty of the scheme became visible. He would beckon to *her* whenever she appeared on the other side of the road, creep up behind her and whisper: 'You're bloody late,' and wait for the reaction. What was it Wellington or Napoleon said? 'Attack is the best means of defence.' Whoever said it was right. Percy sat down and ate a hearty breakfast for the first time in weeks.

It was such a relief to know he was on the attack and not running any more. That morning he caught the eight-thirty to Waterloo and had the satisfaction of spotting his quarry the moment he entered the compartment. Doris was sitting in her usual place by the window. Of course, the sight of his late wife sitting in a train still had the immediate effect of sending icy shivers running down his spine, but, remembering his resolve, he mastered these cowardly emotions and sank down in a seat opposite. Doris treated him to a cold stare in which could be detected a hint of impatience. Percy smiled and felt very confident. He raised his hat and said: 'Morning, Doris. Sorry if I've kept you waiting.'

It was not perhaps the happiest of remarks, because he *was* keeping her waiting, and she stressed her disapproval by turning her head and staring out of the window. Percy did not allow this action to deter him. He felt like a boy who has just left school and can now cheek the master.

'You'll never guess what I did last night. Spilt tea all over your best table-cloth. You know, the one your mother gave us.'

Her face betrayed no sign that she had heard him, but he saw one hand tighten up into a fist. His imagination took flight and he leapt from one outrageous lie to another.

'Do you remember how you used to nag me whenever I cracked a plate? There's not much left of the willow-pattern dinner service. Two vegetable dishes and a meat dish, as a matter of fact, and one lid among the lot.'

Her head quivered, a clenched fist moved, but that was all. He went one, earth-shaking step further.

'The cat hasn't half made a mess of the Indian bedspread.'

The head jerked round, and never would he have thought it possible that a face which was so dead, so white and devoid of emotion, could portray such a picture of blazing, impotent rage. He felt like a man who has been tormenting a caged lion – only some kind of invisible bars kept her at bay.

But instead of fear, he experienced a surge of triumphant joy. She was dead, he was alive and intended to remain so, and he could say anything he damn well liked. He stared straight at her and poked his tongue out. Doris unclenched her fists and once again turned her face to the window.

Percy would have liked to have continued his lion-baiting, but it was then he became aware that several people were looking at him in the oddest way. So he unfolded his newspaper and contented himself by watching Doris over it, just in case she tried to do something tricky. When the train rattled into Waterloo, he opened the carriage door and, after making a little ironic bow, said softly: 'After you.'

She climbed down on to the platform with head held high,

shoulders stiffly erect, and began to walk swiftly towards the ticket barrier, with Percy close behind. He enlivened their progress by such remarks as: 'Gee-up, there's going to be a flood,' 'Watch it, you've got two left feet,' and, when she quickened her pace, 'Hold it, you've forgotten your saddle.'

Once past the ticket barrier she broke into a run and Percy, after emitting a little cry of joy, galloped after her. They both made the lift just before the doors closed, but unfortunately a fat man squeezed between them, so that Percy was unable to continue his exorcizing treatment. When the crowd swept out into the lower regions, where passage meets passage in the midst of a mind-numbing labyrinth, Percy found he had lost his prey. He looked, stretched his neck, struggled, elbowed and finally shouted. All to no avail. She had vanished. The heat had become too hot in the kitchen and Doris had got out.

Percy, to the profound enjoyment of all those in his immediate vicinity, laughed, danced, swore and finally cried. It was reasonable to suppose that the attack procedure was an unqualified success.

Percy found his day was packed with hours that were reluctant to die. Sometimes he chuckled when he realized how his feelings regarding Doris's post-demise wanderings had been reversed. Now he would be extremely disappointed if she were not on the homeward-bound train. He devised new insults, invented little acts of ridicule, that must surely rouse her to a state of impotent rage. But of course he must never lower his guard: always make certain she was in front and he was in the rear.

When the first shadows of night fell across the city, Percy Fortesque put on his coat and hat, gathered up his briefcase and umbrella, then set forth to renew the hunt. Doris was not on the Piccadilly Line, and he experienced a twinge of disappointment. Neither, so far as he could see, was she on the Bakerloo train, but the crowd was so dense that an entire army of ghosts could be flattened between strap-hanging bodies, or whimpering against doors. With many a look to the rear, Percy hastened to the lift and gave a little squeal of alarm when a woman in a blue hat pressed her handbag into his back. But it was not Doris, and he came up into the main station without so much as a glimpse of his quarry.

The five-forty-five was still only half filled, so Percy was able to examine each compartment without difficulty. He found her at the far end of the train, huddled against the off-side window, head averted, shoulders hunched, looking like a badly-wrapped parcel that someone had forgotten. He climbed in, put his umbrella and briefcase up on the luggage rack, then sat down beside her.

'Evening.' He kept his voice low. 'Thought I'd missed you.'

There was no response – he did not expect one.

'Why did you run away this morning? That wasn't a nice thing to do, was it? I've got so much to say, and you never gave me much opportunity to talk when you were alive. For example, I never did mention how much I hated you, although, to be fair, I did not realize it myself at the time. I only knew you were mean, small-minded, sanctimonious, petty and an awful person to live with. Are you listening?'

The back of her neck was more waxlike than ever and he felt a sudden surge of anger. She was treating him with contempt. His words – his feelings – were not worthy of her attention. He raised his voice slightly.

'Why did I marry you? Eh! Didn't you ever ask yourself that question once in all those years? I'll tell you. I thought that anyone so unattractive – I could use the word ugly – would always be grateful. I overlooked the undeniable fact that women only look into rose-tinted mirrors.' He drew a little nearer and turned his voice into a harsh, vibrant whisper. 'Get back to hell, you ugly old cow.'

She still did not move, but her whisper thundered through the dark corridors of his mind.

'My mother is only two carriages back.'

He became aware that the train had already begun its journey towards Richmond and the living people (so far as he knew) had filled every seat and overflowed into the aisles, but he was now more alone than at any time during his life. He wondered what would be the reaction if he were to jump up and shout: 'That thing in the corner – it's my dead wife.' Would they all gape at him, or – and this was a chilling thought – just nod their heads and say: 'Yes, we know'? If his mother-in-law – may she burn forever – was two carriages back, what proof had he that all of them were not dead as a Christmas turkey? Hell below! – all fourteen stone of the old hag had been planted in Brookwood cemetery twenty-five years ago. He shuddered and looked at his nearest neighbours with terrible suspicion. That fat man who was propped up against the far door looked unpleasantly waxy. And that long, lean woman with protruding teeth, she might well have strayed from some far-off damp grave. Then bravado, the dire need to drive fear back behind the frontiers of sanity, made him turn to Doris again.

'Let the old hag come. I'll settle her hash, too. Dead or alive, it's all the same to me. Let 'em all come.'

Silence. Rigid immobility. Fired by a childish and, by now, terror-tinted fear, Percy would have liked to have punched that motionless figure. But once, when his knee touched hers, there was such a bone-chilling coldness, he slumped back against the same dour-faced woman from whom he had received warning frowns on earlier occasions.

'Kindly desist,' she instructed, pulling her skirt abruptly away as though to avoid contamination.

'It was only my intention ...'

'I know exactly what your intention was. Kindly desist.'

Every *supposed* living body looked at Percy, but Doris continued to ignore him, although there was something about the way she held her head and shoulders that stated more eloquently than looks or words that this was the kind of reputation that she fully endorsed. When the train reached Richmond, he edged his way from the compartment with lowered head and did not wait to see if Doris's mother was on the look-out for him.

That night he did not sleep much, but spent the small hours feeding his courage. He rehearsed all the cutting remarks he would make to Doris's mother, should she put in an appearance next morning. Then he remembered the formidable bulk, the immense, moonlike face, and hastily turned on the bedside lamp.

'She won't scare me!' he shouted, and the cat, which had been sleeping on the foot of the bed, beat a hasty retreat.

Doris was back in her customary position by the window and

Percy, true to his newly-acquired determination, sat down beside her. He asked the all-important question.

'All right. Where is the old hag?'

It is a pity that he had not looked to left and right when he entered the compartment, because Doris's mother was seated opposite. He said: 'Oh, my God,' and stared at her with open mouth and bulging eyes. She really was most awful. A great round face, endowed with three chins, little eyes that glittered from behind horn-rimmed spectacles, shoulders that would not have disgraced a coal-heaver, a bosom that verged on the impossible, and legs like miniature tree-trunks. She wore a black straw hat, a grey coat with a moth-blitzed fur collar and a pair of buttoned-up boots. To make matters worse she did not look out of the window. The small, unblinking eyes magnified by the spectacles, stared straight at Percy, the dead-white face wore an expression of frozen disapproval and the overall impression was that of a corpse that had died while in a fit of excessive bad-temper. Percy stared back until his self-control exploded into an eruption of terror-born rage.

'Who do you think you're staring at?'

What with one thing and another, Percy was becoming a source of entertainment for bored commuters. Newspapers rustled, heads were raised, dull eyes brightened and there was a general air of lively excitement. But Percy's mother-in-law did not appear to be impressed. She remained a solid, motionless, larger-than-life wax doll, and her magnified stare never left Percy's face. He might have spoken again, had he not been forestalled by a sudden low whisper. It came from Doris, who was still indulging her passion for looking out of train windows.

'Daddy is in the guard's van.'

Percy sank back and closed his eyes. Despair came strolling down the avenues of time and took up residence in Percy's brain. It banished hope with a hollow laugh, slaughtered confidence with a tiny frown and welcomed horror with a grisly smile.

Percy knew he had lost.

Doris allowed someone to open the door before slowly descending to the platform. There she stood waiting, and

Percy, after a fearful glance at his mother-in-law, knew what was expected of him. Presently there were a compact family group, with wife in front, husband behind, mother-in-law to the left and father-in-law moving in.

Doris's father had been a very large man and was in every way a worthy spouse for his formidable partner. Six-foot-four high, by three-foot-six wide, he had a face of granite and fists like bunches of iron grapes. He gave the impression he was looking for someone to hit. He took up a position to Percy's right and the family group moved forward.

Through the ticket barrier, across the station, down the steps and into the lift. Here Percy surrendered his season ticket. He would be travelling free from now on. On the Bakerloo platform they allowed one train to come and go, but looked grimly at Percy when the second announced its imminent arrival by a fast growing roar. Percy trembled and closed his eyes and from somewhere close behind came a nasty little tittering laugh. The roar exploded into a shriek of triumph as the train was vomited out of the tunnel mouth and father-in-law's voice rumbled as he spoke the fatal words.

'Over you go and happy landing.'

They all shoved together.

Percy found himself in a corner seat and he was looking miserably out of the window. The train was just drawing into Charing Cross station. It was then that he turned his head and took an interest in his surroundings. Mother-in-law and father-in-law were seated opposite, Doris was on his left. They were all smirking and resembled three cats preparing to share out one mouse. Percy ventured to ask a question.

'Where are we going?'

'To Leicester Square,' said Doris.

'Then change for King's Cross,' added father-in-law.

'For a nice trip to Walthamstow Central,' mother-in-law stated.

'And back to Finsbury Park,' said Doris.

'Then up to Cockfosters.'

'Back to Hyde Park Corner.'

'We'll spend the night in the Victoria Station first-class waiting-room,' promised father-in-law.

People poured in from the platform, seats were crowded, overhead straps sagged under the weight of hangers-on, aisles were packed solid with homeward-bound (or was it work-bound?) commuters, and demons disguised as porters glared in through the grime-fogged windows.

'It's always the rush hour,' said Doris.

'Eternally,' added father-in-law.

Mother-in-law had the last word. She always had.

'For ever and ever.'